The Story of the Movie

Adapted by G. M. Berrow

Based on a Screenplay written by
Meghan McCarthy, Rita Hsiao and
Michael Vogel

ORCHARD

Contents

Prologue

In the magical land of Equestria, there lived four powerful pony princesses. There was one for the day, one for the night, one for family and, last but not least, one to represent the magic of a force greater than any other – friendship. The last pony was named Princess Twilight Sparkle and she was incredibly special.

Although Twilight Sparkle was the newest princess in the land, everypony knew that she was wise beyond her years. However, Princess Twilight herself acknowledged that she still had much to learn. But luckily, lessons were not just a very serious business to her – they were everything. In fact, that's how Twilight already had come to understand that it was her supreme royal duty to make everypony feel like they belonged.

Thanks to her amazing friends, Twilight felt that she was well prepared to meet whatever friendship challenge lay ahead of her and the citizens of Equestria. Pinkie Pie, Rarity, Rainbow Dash, Fluttershy and Applejack would be there for Twilight – no matter what!

Twilight's greatest wish for every single pony in Equestria was that they would experience the magic of a friendship like the one she shared with her friends. It was such a relief to have somepony with which to laugh, share time, practise loyalty, show kindness and lend an honest opinion. Twilight Sparkle felt that sometimes being a princess could feel like quite a lot of pressure. But as long as Princess Twilight had her friends and a well-thought-out plan, she knew, deep in her royal heart, that she would be the princess everypony needed her to be.

But even the ever-prepared Princess Twilight would soon learn a new lesson – there were simply some things that nopony could plan for …

CHAPTER 1

Prepare for the Festival

The painted purple and pink sunrise melted into cool, breezy blue skies as ponies from all over Equestria journeyed towards the bustling epicentre of Canterlot. Hundreds of winged Pegasi soared through the fluffy clouds up above. Down below, the Unicorns and Earth ponies journeyed by train, cart and hoof from the far reaches of the kingdom.

The excitement about the event was so palpable that it seemed like it was buzzing through the air in little shockwaves. Some ponies even felt butterflies in their tummies and sweet songs on their lips as they anticipated all of the fun and friendship they were going to experience at the very first Festival of Friendship. Anything could happen!

The busy streets were already starting to fill up as Spike, the young dragon who was the best friend (and advisor) to the Princess of Friendship pushed his way through the gathering crowds with urgency. "Excuse me!" he called out, struggling to keep hold of the armloads of important scrolls he was taking to the princess. "Dragon on the move! Comin' through! Watch your tail!" Ponies darted out of the way to accommodate him, whispering with excitement as he passed.

"What do you even DO at a Friendship Festival?" an Earth pony with red pigtails asked in awe as she took in the glorious scene around her.

"Make friends, bond over music … meet all four princesses?" a golden-coloured mare with a honey pot cutie mark replied as they trotted off to find out.

Spike mentally took note of their

excited comments so he could relay to Princess Twilight just how wonderful an idea the whole festival had been. It hadn't even started yet, but it was already a hit! Spike just knew it was going to be thrilling – he had a feeling in his gut.

The little dragon continued across the

cobblestone square with his scrolls and a smug hop in his steps. He was so distracted he almost walked right into another pair of overexcited filly Pegasi flying right past him and up into the air. Their giggles of delight were even louder than the ponies jumping in the bouncy castle.

"Do you think they'll let me wear their crowns?" wondered a lilac filly named Violet Petals as she soared high above Canterlot to get a better view.

Her friend grinned. "I bet Princess Twilight is the most perfect pony EVER!"

It seemed everypony had the beloved princesses on their minds. In addition to the appearance of the four royal princesses, there were going to be so many exciting things to see! But the true 'mane event' of the weekend would be the stunning musical styling of the talented

Songbird Serenade. The pop star was set to perform in an epic show that would undoubtedly go down in Equestrian history as one of the best of all time. Or it might not. It depended whether or not Twilight could convince the other princesses to go along with her ingenious plan to enhance the experience for everypony in the audience.

But not everypony was feeling great. Up in the castle, Twilight paced tirelessly back and forth. She couldn't stop fretting over the fact that every detail of the occasion had to be just perfect. After all, everypony's happiness rested in Twilight's hooves! She couldn't let them down.

Taking a cue from her own serene image depicted in the stained glass windows, Twilight paused and spread her majestic purple wings out wide. She took a deep breath to summon her courage and centre her thoughts. Twilight held the air in her lungs for a moment. *Just go in there and ask*, she told herself. *This is YOUR friendship festival.*

She expelled the air in a heavy sigh and shook her head in frustration. "Nope! Still worried. Oooh … nothing is working!" She let her face fall into her hoof and scrunched up her muzzle. Luckily, she was pulled from her thoughts by a friendly voice.

"OK, Twilight!" Spike scrambled inside the cavernous hall with a smile on his face. He was still buzzing from all the activity outside. "I've got all your charts and graphs!" The dragon carried his mountain of scrolls to the princess.

"Oh, thank goodness you're here, Spike!" Twilight called out. "I'm just so nervous about this meeting."

"Just remember the most important thing," he told her.

"To smile?" Twilight twisted her face into a forced version of a grin.

"Uh, no …" he replied, a little scared by her face. "That you have a plan."

"Yes, that's true," Twilight nodded. Of course Spike was right. Twilight had prepared for this and there was nothing to be afraid of. The other three princesses were practically her family. Whatever she had to say, they would listen. Twilight was ready. She nodded at Spike and stepped through the massive double doors to the throne room.

"Wish me luck!"

CHAPTER 2
The Magic You Need

The three other royals listened intently as Twilight enthusiastically bounded back and forth in front of a large whiteboard, which showed an illustration of the performance stage alongside several advanced friendship equations. If Twilight could get the other princesses to agree to this minor adjustment, it would ensure that the Friendship Festival would be the most wonderful event that Equestria had ever seen!

"Songbird Serenade's performance is not scheduled to start until after you begin the sunset, and based on my precise calculation, to get the very best lighting for the stage …" Twilight looked to Princess Celestia. "I was hoping you could make sure the sun stays about twenty-eight point one degrees to the south," Twilight said as she drew a little Celestia on the board underneath a picture of the sun. Her voice seemed to speed up once she got started.

"And Princess Luna, if you could raise the moon sixty-two degrees to the north at the same time, it would reflect the sunlight on the other side perfectly!"

Twilight drew
a picture of
Luna under
the
moon
and an
acute angle
to prove that her
theory was sound.

Princess Celestia and Luna looked at one another in disbelief. Why did their Princess Twilight stress herself out over such minor details? Luna opened her mouth to reply to the proposal but Twilight wasn't finished just yet.

"And Cadance, if you could use your crystal magic to create an aurora above the stage, the sun AND the moon would shine through it and create a truly amazing light show!"

As Twilight spoke her final words, Spike threw a clawful of glitter up into the air. It swirled down as if it were a beautiful aurora. Spike then poked a hoof-made paper puppet of the pop star above the whiteboard and made it dance. "Presenting: Songbird Serenade! Yaaaa, yaaah! Whoaa ho ho!" Spike leapt on top of the board for emphasis, but quickly lost his balance. The dragon came tumbling to the ground.

Twilight blushed at Spike's awkward display and opened her wings to block the princesses' view of him. She flashed a toothy smile to finish her brilliant presentation. Any minute now they would congratulate her and ...

"So, you're saying you want us to move the sun and the moon ..." Princess Luna recapped, a hesitant look on her face.

"All for the party?"

"Well, I'd do it myself," Twilight laughed nervously. "But I don't have your magic!"

It was difficult to gauge their thoughts, but the fact that all three princesses stepped forwards with her their horns glowing gave Twilight a little glimmer of hope. But

Princess Celestia just frowned. "Twilight, each of us uses our powers to serve Equestria in our own way." Celestia's face softened as she reached for Twilight's chin with her gold-plated hoof. "You are the Princess of Friendship! You already have all the magic you need."

"So … is that a no?" Twilight sighed in defeat. How was she going to make the festival special now? She could feel her disappointment sinking in, but before it had the chance, her trusty pal Spike snapped to action. He pushed her out of the throne room. After all, they had a checklist to get to, and ponies to see. There was no time to waste today!

Everypony was waiting for her.

CHAPTER 3

We Got This

The last few stubborn clouds above Canterlot were obliterated with a single swoop from Rainbow Dash. The Pegasus sped through each one with glee and watched as her rainbow trail broke through the mist. Rainbow Dash loved clearing the skies, but she loved helping her friends even more. To be able to do both at once was her favourite thing!

"Skies cleared and ready for the festival!" Rainbow Dash announced with satisfaction.

She took off towards the main square, where a vast amphitheatre was being decorated for the evening's events. Maybe somepony needed a hoof with something else!

"That looks awesome, Pinkie!" Rainbow shouted as she swooped past Pinkie Pie. The pink party pony was busy blowing up balloons and twisting them into fun shapes. Pinkie took a deep breath and blew into a red balloon with all her might. It inflated quickly and a few seconds later, turned into a perfect likeness of Discord. But before she could admire her hoofiwork, the balloon sprang a leak and shot off into the distance.

"Heads up! RUNAWAY BALLOON!" Pinkie squealed as she bounded after it, straight past Fluttershy, who was busy preparing for the festival. The sweet yellow Pegasus spun around in surprise as her singing flock of chorus birds took flight in every direction.

Nearby, Applejack was busy hauling her apple juice cart through the courtyard, giving out free samples to anypony she came across. After passing out a few mugs to grateful ponies, she trotted over to the stage area to check on its progress.

Unsurprisingly, Rarity was keeping herself busy by delicately hanging bows along the edge. After she tied each one, she used her magic to place a beautiful gem in the centre of it. The stage was

beginning to look exactly as Rarity hoped
it would – perfect.

"Wow, Rarity, that's a fine job you're
doin' there!"

Applejack shouted
to her meticulous
friend. "Course, it
might not get done 'til
after the concert!"
Rarity had only hung
about three bows so far.

"Applejack, darling, anypony can do a
'fine' job," Rarity turned her nose up and
closed her eyes. "Twilight asked me to help,
so clearly she's going for fabulous! And
fabulous takes time …" The unicorn got
back to work, carefully tying the next bow
with love.

"Fabulous takes for ever!" Rainbow
Dash butted in as she landed near

Applejack. "But 'awesome'? That can get done in four seconds flat!" Before Rarity could protest, Rainbow Dash darted over to her and grabbed the ribbons and gems. She zoomed around the stage in the blink of an eye. When the ponies looked again, the entire thing was finished!

"I could do it even faster if I did my Sonic Rainboom …" Rainbow Dash said, proudly. But it looked awful. The bows drooped and gems were misplaced.

Rarity cried out in despair. How was she going to fix this mess in time? "No, no, no! Don't you dare! It looks wretched enough already—"

Rainbow Dash shrugged. "Oh, come on, it looks fine."

"If you were raised in a barn!" Rarity huffed. "No offence, Applejack."

"None taken!" Applejack laughed and

kept pouring mugs of juice. Her family just happened to have a barn. Where she was born. And spent most of her formative years …

Rarity rushed over to the mess and began to fix it. Fluttershy and Pinkie Pie trotted up to help, but before they could, everypony noticed that Twilight and Spike were approaching. They were hiding behind a huge scroll with a checklist on it, which meant their friends were probably at peak pre-event stress levels.

"Hey, Twilight!" everypony chorused cheerily.

Rarity smiled at the little dragon. "Hello, Spike …" Spike waved back and blushed pink with embarrassment. After all this time, he still had a crush on the glamorous Unicorn.

"How'd it go with the other princesses?" Applejack smiled brightly. "They like your idea?"

"Not exactly." Twilight sighed heavily, reliving the meeting and feeling just as bad all over again. "They think I can make today perfect without their magic."

"And they are absolutely right, darling!" Rarity moved closer to Twilight. She just needed some extra support. "This festival is your brilliant idea, and we all know you're up to the task!" Rarity reassured her.

Twilight bit her lip, unconvinced. But what if she wasn't? What if Songbird Serenade hated the stage? Or nopony made a new friend? If she failed at the festival, then who was she? Not the Princess of Friendship, that's for sure.

"Twilight!" Pinkie Pie bounded over and took Twilight's face in her hooves. "Look at me!" Pinkie's stare was all sorts of intense and her bushy  fuchsia mane sprang out wildly. "This will be the biggest celebration Equestria has ever seen! You CANNOT fail. The pressure is INTENSE! It's almost too much for any single pony to handle!" Pinkie squealed. She really wasn't helping Twilight's nerves.

"… But you have us!" Pinkie said with a cheesy smile. She gestured round to Rainbow Dash, Fluttershy, Rarity and

Applejack. "So stop worrying."

Twilight's friends gathered around her and enveloped her in a group hug. "WE GOT THIS!" they all shouted together before erupting into a fit of giggles. Twilight couldn't help smiling. With the help of her friends, she'd have no problem getting everything just right. All they had to do was make it fun!

Applejack started to hum a tune. Soon enough, everypony was singing along together as they worked to get everything ready – from the epic stage to the decorations, the food and the games.

"We got this ... we got this together!" Twilight sang along as she trotted past the booths. It was finally beginning to feel like the forecast would be nothing but sunny skies and a perfect festival when all of a sudden ...

SPLAT! Twilight found herself covered with a gigantic sugary, fluffy … *cake?*

"PINKIE!" Twilight whined, stepping out of the gooey mess. Dollops of icing and sprinkles slid down her mane and wings, and a single lit birthday candle landed precisely on her horn.

"Oopsie! Guess my easy-bake confetti-cake cannon needs a little fine-tuning!" Pinkie laughed, popping out of a giant contraption. The crowd of ponies who had gathered around gasped in shock.

But the glances and gasps weren't directed at Twilight at all – they were for somepony even more special. The star of the show! Songbird Serenade had arrived – and Princess Twilight Sparkle was covered in cake!

CHAPTER 4

Unexpected Weather

"Songbird Serenade! She's here!" the
ponies whispered in awe as the crowd
parted to make way for the singer. Her
two bodyguard stallions, outfitted in dark
jackets and sunglasses, trotted ahead in
an attempt to clear the path even more.
Then they puffed up their chests with a

sense of pride and stepped aside. There she was!

The pop diva, a buttercream-coloured Earth pony, wore her signature mane style in black and yellow choppy locks that hung directly over her eyes. She had a large pink bow behind her head and a black jacket that was effortlessly cool. Everypony always loved how mysterious her edgy look made her seem.

"Hiya!" Songbird chirped in a sweet voice. "I'm looking for the pony in charge?" She looked around at the masses of gawking ponies, scanning the crowd aimlessly. "I need to set up for my sound check?"

"Songbird Serenade?" Twilight stepped forward, feeling a bit starstruck. But clearly she should be the one to handle this. On top of everything else. "Um, I was just going to check on you – I'm Princess Twilight!" A blob of cake slid down her shoulder. Suddenly Twilight was aware of how odd her current state must look to her guest. "And sorry about the mess! Usually, I'm not so—"

Twilight gestured and a drop of batter managed to fling itself right on to Songbird Serenade. "Caked in ... cake?" She laughed as her bodyguard wiped it away. Now Twilight was officially embarrassed. What else could go wrong today?

A low rumble rang out and a mass of black and grey started to appear in the sky. "Storm clouds?" cried Twilight. All of the good feelings from the past hour were dissipating. "But I ordered perfect weather!" She looked to Rainbow Dash in confusion. The Pegasi supposedly had been working non-stop to make sure no weather catastrophes would ruin their day. "Rainbow Dash?"

"Uh, I ..." Rainbow Dash's voice quavered. "I don't think those are storm clouds ..." The masses of ponies watched in bewilderment as a giant airship burst through the darkened mist and into the atmosphere. It was shaped like a giant egg, only it was wooden underneath, like the hull of a boat. There were sharp, angular propellers jutting out from the back and a rudder below. It was most unusual.

"Oooh!" said Pinkie Pie with glee. "I bet those are the clowns I ordered!"

But as the ship landed on the square, it began to crush everything in its wake, including several of the tall spires that bore Canterlot's flags. Ponies galloped out of the way to make room for the monstrosity. And Pinkie Pie came to the realisation that the scary airship was definitely not holding the clowns she had ordered.

It was something sinister.

Twilight narrowed her eyes, trying to make sense of what was happening. She had a horrible feeling, but felt powerless. She didn't even know who these visitors were – so how could she stop them? Up on the castle balcony, the other princesses experienced the same sinking sensation.

A door on the hull opened and gangway unfurled itself. Silhouetted in its frame was a small, squat creature.

His name was Grubber.
From his pallid, grey skin
to his pig-like nose, up to
his white, spiky hair and
right to the tips of his
pointy claws, he was an
unusual sight. Grubber
hoisted a large box in front of him and
made his way down the gangway towards
the ponies, trying to look as intimidating
as possible.

Once he'd arrived, Grubber made a
big show about pushing a button to open
the box. Everypony held their breath as
the box grew into a giant, mechanical
megaphone. Grubber held the cone up to
his mouth with satisfaction and
summoned the scariest voice he could.

"Ponies of Equestria ... we come on
behalf of the fearsome, the powerful, the

almighty ... Storm King!" Grubber gestured to the ship dramatically and a giant poster unfurled itself. On it was a terrifying, horned beast with icy blue eyes. An emblem emblazoned on his chest looked like two sharp spikes. Nothing about this intrusion seemed friendly. The ponies erupted into a wave of panicked whispers.

"And now, to deliver his evil, evil message: put your hooves together for COMMANDER TEMPEST!" Grubber looked ecstatic as he gestured with his stubby arm t the door and stepped aside to make way for his superior.

The striking Unicorn stepped forward to reveal herself. Tempest's dark purple hide and cropped scarlet mane matched her intimidating black armour. A mysterious scar ran across one of her teal-coloured eyes. But the strangest feature of all was her horn.

It was broken.

Twilight Sparkle gasped. She'd never seen anypony's horn jutting out into shards like that before. Something horrible had happened to Tempest, and Twilight found herself wondering what it was.

"Tempest, is it?" Princess Celestia's gentle, yet commanding voice rang out as the three remaining princesses soared down from the castle balcony to greet the intruders. "How may we help you?"

"Ah, I'm so glad you asked." Tempest smirked. Her voice dripped with sarcasm. "How about we start with your complete and total surrender?"

CHAPTER 5
Attack on Canterlot

Twilight pushed past the other ponies and stepped forward to line up with Princesses Celestia, Luna and Cadance. There had to be a diplomatic way to solve this little misunderstanding. All it would take was a friendly conversation and they'd be back to getting ready for the festival of friendship.

"Hello there! Princess of Friendship here …" Twilight tried to catch Tempest's eyes. When she did, she felt an icy chill go down her spine. "… Not exactly sure what's going on, but I know we can talk things out." Twilight gave Tempest her friendliest smile. It always worked.

But Tempest just chuckled. "Oh, goodie. All four princesses!" Tempest started down the gangway, slamming her hooves on the metal planks with confidence. "Here's the deal, ladies – I need your magic. Give it up nicely, please, or we'll make it difficult." Tempest shot Twilight a pointed look. "For everyone."

"And why exactly should we cower before you?" Princess Luna shot back. "There's one of you, and hundreds of us!" Luna gestured to the crowd of ponies behind her, who all puffed out their chests and stood a little taller in support.

Tempest was unfazed. The evil unicorn let out a low chuckle. "I was hoping you'd choose ... difficult."

Out of nowhere, dozens more strange airships appeared in the sky! Hordes of enormous, yeti-like creatures wearing the Storm King's emblem came leaping out of their ships. They grunted and growled as they landed all over the square. The ponies screamed in horror as they ran for cover. Canterlot was under attack!

Princess Cadance sprang into action, lunging towards Tempest's ship. But she was too late. Tempest jumped into the air, spun around and kicked something with her back hoof. The glowing orb shot straight to Cadance. She was able to block it with her magic shield, but the orb was too strong. It lingered, frozen right in front of Princess Cadance's face as she fought to hold it back.

"I can't … stop it!" Cadance cried out. A moment later, the orb had worked its evil magic, turning her completely to stone. Twilight gasped in horror as Celestia cried out for her fallen comrade.

"Luna! Quick!" Celestia shouted to her sister. "Go South! Beyond the badlands! Seek help from the Queen of the Hippo—"

But before she could finish her sentence, Tempest had thrown another orb right at the princesses. "Nooooo!" Twilight shouted, helpless as stone

engulfed Celestia's body. Now she too had
become a statue with her face contorted
into a permanent expression of horror.
Luna took off into the air, swerving
between the airships to escape and carry
out Celestia's
instructions.

But it was in
vain, because
Tempest was
already a step
ahead of Luna.
She produced two
more green orbs and
jumped into the air
again, kicking one right at
Luna. When it hit her wing, the princess
lost control. Luna tumbled back to the
ground, and by the time she'd reached it,
she was completely frozen in stone.

Twilight couldn't believe her eyes. All three of the other princesses were immobilised. "Nooooo!" she couldn't help crying out in agony.

Tempest cackled, zeroing in on Twilight. One more princess to go before she had what she needed to please the Storm King. She watched as the sweet purple princess was overcome with emotion. Too simple.

It was the perfect time to strike. Tempest hurled the last orb at the pony with unbridled glee. Green smoke and rainbows burst forth, obstructing the view as they hit the sad little pony.

"Easy as pie," Tempest mumbled to herself with a certain smugness.

"Oh, I love pie," added Grubber.

The smoke cleared and Tempest trotted up to the pony frozen in place.

Grubber scrambled over and leaned in close to look at her horn. But it wasn't a horn at all – it was a party hat! This pony was a cross-eyed Pegasus with a cutie mark of bubbles.

"That's not the princess!" Tempest growled. Her horn sputtered and sparked with magical rage. "Grubber ... Get. Her. NOW!" Grubber panicked and took off towards the edge of the courtyard, to where Storm Creatures were lunging after a group of ponies.

"Over here, y'all!" Applejack shouted, leading the way.

Rainbow Dash darted ahead. "Come on!" Fluttershy, Rarity, Pinkie Pie and Twilight galloped after them, darting out of the path of the terrifying Storm Creatures until they found themselves cornered on a bridge.

In a moment of quick thinking, Twilight fired a magic beam directly at the Storm Creature. He lifted his shield. The magic bounced back and shot directly at the ground. The ponies gasped as a crack began to form in the stone bridge. It was crumbling right beneath their hooves!

The bridge gave way, taking all six ponies down with it. They screamed as they plunged into the rushing water below. The ponies bobbed to the surface, paddling their hooves and gasping for air, but the current was too strong.

They were headed right for a steep waterfall and there was no way to stop it or change their path. "Ahhhhh!!" the friends screamed in unison as they plummeted over the waterfall!

CHAPTER 6

In This Together

The ponies took shelter in a tiny cave
next to the river below Canterlot.
Everypony was wet and bedraggled,
but seemed to be all right. "Is everypony
OK?" Applejack asked as she fished her
soaking cowpony hat out of the water.
The limp brown brim dripped on to
her mane.

"Well, they were the worst party crashers EVER!" Pinkie Pie marvelled. She wrung her curly mane and a bucket's worth of water came pouring out.

Everypony agreed, but nopony could decide on what their best next course of action would be. Rainbow Dash wanted to go back and fight, but Spike insisted that the sheer size of the Storm Creatures would make it impossible. Always the practical one, Applejack pointed out that they had to decide quickly – they couldn't just stay in this cave for ever. And they couldn't let Tempest find Twilight. As discussion turned to theories on what might have happened to the evil Unicorn's broken horn, Twilight trotted to the water's edge to think.

Everything had come crashing down so fast. What was she supposed to do now? The kingdom was under attack and she was the only princess who'd escaped. It was up to her to rescue everypony! It had all happened so fast! Twilight thought back through the events, and then suddenly she remembered a clue.

Celestia had been telling Luna to seek help from somepony. "The queen ..." Twilight mumbled to herself.

"Yeah, the queen!" chirped Pinkie Pie, then her face fell. "Uh ... what queen?"

"The Queen of the ... Hippos?" Twilight replied. When she said it out loud, it sounded ridiculous even to her.

"Hippos?" Rainbow Dash scoffed. "Seriously?"

Twilight nodded. "They're somewhere South, past the badlands. We have to go there and get help."

Fluttershy cowered. "But that means

we'll have to …
leave Equestria!"
Her voice was so
tiny it was
practically a squeak.
"I'm not even
packed!" Rarity
whimpered, thinking of all
the situations she might find herself in
without the proper outfit. She shuddered.

"I understand you're scared. And
nopony else has to go …" Twilight
replied. She glanced up to the sky where
the airships were still hovering. It made
her stomach lurch to think of the citizens
left up there. "But I have to find this
queen. She might be our only hope to
save Equestria." Twilight took a deep
breath and turned on her hoof to leave.
She had no choice. If her friends couldn't

come, she would just have to go it alone.

"Well, you're not getting all the glory!" Rainbow Dash chimed in. "We're in this together!" The rainbow Pegasus flew over to Twilight and gave her an encouraging smile. The others gathered around and nodded in agreement.

The princess felt a wave of relief wash over her as she realised her friends were all going to be with her along the journey. She hadn't let herself admit that she had been scared to be alone. Now all they had to do was find which direction was South.

"Uh … that way?" Spike pointed his claw towards the edge of a forest, thick with wide-trunked trees.

"Let's go find this Hippo." *Boingy! Boingy! Boingy!* Pinkie Pie bounced over in her signature style and took the lead. "Hey – anypony up for a game of 'I Spy'?"

The others groaned and trotted after her, bracing themselves for the potentially long journey ahead. At least they had each other.

Chapter 7
The Staff of Sacanas

Back in Canterlot, things were worse than even Twilight could imagine. The Storm Creature warriors had rounded up everypony in the whole capital into groups, and then they'd shackled their hooves together. As the Storm King's prisoners, the little ponies were all forced to march back and forth endlessly.

It was simply miserable.

Tempest had taken up residence in the castle. She watched the activity from the balcony, thinking of all the changes that would have to be made to this city once the Storm King finally arrived to take power. Remnants of the Friendship Festival decorations still littered the sparkled cobblestone streets, and colourful balloons floated into the air. It was too happy.

"All this power," Tempest mumbled in disgust as a bunch of rainbow-coloured balloons floated past her perch. "Wasted on parties, when there are far greater uses." Tempest could feel the anger rising inside her as she caught sight of her reflection in a pane of glass. Her broken horn stared back at her, useless. Tempest pushed her feelings down, rolled her eyes

and trotted back inside the castle. There
was work to do.

One of the Storm Creatures
approached Tempest. He reached out his
claws to her and presented a round glass
bottle filled with a glowing liquid. It
pulsated with light and emitted a watery,
high-pitched sound that echoed through
the cavernous hall.

"Well, answer it!" Tempest barked.
Sometimes, she couldn't help feeling like
she was surrounded by incompetent oafs.
They couldn't even accomplish the
simplest tasks, like answering a potion
call. The Storm Creature fumbled to
uncork the bottle and poured it into
a large basin. Instantly, the liquid shot
up into a vapoury cylinder. And in the
mist, the image of the Storm King
appeared!

The frightening beast spun around in confusion. "Where am I supposed to be looking? I never understand how this spell works. TEMPEST!" the Storm King growled.

"Over here, Your Excellency," Tempest said patiently. She was used to her boss relying on her to accomplish even the smallest things. The Storm King was still spinning around, unable to locate her. "Over here, look to your right."

"Oh, there you are. Here's the deal—" The Storm King waved his gnarled wooden staff at her. The crystal embedded at the top glinted in the projection's light. "Going by the name 'The Storm King' is intensely intimidating and everything, but you know what? I need to back it up!" He sneered. "You know what I need to back it up with? A STORM!" His icy blue eyes bore into Tempest's. "You promised me magic that could control the elements and right now I'm holding a what?" The Storm King held up his staff. "A branch, a twig! Blehhh!"

For the hundredth time, Tempest explained to her superior that he was not in fact, holding a twig, but the Staff of Sacanas. The ancient relic would serve as a conduit to channel the magic of the four rulers of Equestria. "You'll soon have the power of a hundred armies," she told him patiently.

The Storm King smirked wickedly. "So that would be a 'yes' on you taking down the four Pegacornicuses or whatever you call them?"

Tempest braced herself to tell him the bad news – she was still missing one princess. They needed all four of the royals for the staff to work, but that sneaky little purple one had got away. Grubber had really messed that one up.

"Give me three days," Tempest decided to say instead of the truth. "I'll have everything ready for your arrival." She bowed to the Storm King and he disappeared into the mist.

Tempest took a deep breath as she realised the challenge ahead of her. She had to find that pony – and fast. Nothing was as important as this. Finding that princess was Tempest's only chance of getting the one thing she desired most, from the only creature that could give it to her. Because once he had the power of Equestria within his control, the Storm King was going to restore Tempest's broken horn and the full powers of her magic would return along with it. Finally.

"Prepare my ship!" Tempest growled at her sidekicks. Her chipped horn sparked with tiny, coloured shocks of lightning. Then she narrowed her eyes, determined. "Please, how far can one little pony get on her own?"

CHAPTER 8

Beware of Klugetown

The ponies were delirious as they trudged through the barren desert landscape, barely moving at all. The hot sun bore down on their hides. They were dusty, achy and so thirsty that that they couldn't remember what water tasted like. Drops of salty sweat poured down their muzzles and their eyes were ringed with the dark circles of deep exhaustion. It felt as if Twilight Sparkle and her friends had been trotting for their whole lives.

"Saving Equestria!" Pinkie Pie laughed to herself maniacally. "Oh look!" She plucked an ancient bird skull from the sand and dust poured from its eye sockets. "Maybe this guy knows which way to go!" Pinkie held the skull to her ear. "What's that? We're lost?" She tossed the skull and erupted into a fit of hysterical giggles before collapsing down into the sandy dune.

Nearby, Spike was struggling with a wayward prickly cactus that had adhered itself to his bottom. "We could be going in circles! Endless sand … nothing for miles but sand …" Spike coughed and sputtered. His throat was so dry. "… And this road."

"A road?" said Twilight Sparkle, perking up. "Where there's a road, there's a …" She trotted forward along, cresting the nearest dune. What she saw next took her breath away. There was a city!

Klugetown was unlike any city Twilight had ever seen, stacked high with dark, smoking spires and foreign buildings. Even the path to the city looked ominous, littered with old wreckage that jutted out from the sand. But it was something.

"Oooh! A city!" Pinkie Pie bounded forward with renewed energy. "We are DOING IT, you guys!" she squealed in delight. The other ponies rushed forward to join

them, wondering aloud what sort of place the city might be. Rarity was hoping for a spa, but everypony else was just eager to rest, find some food and gather information on where to find the Queen of the Hippos.

But as soon as they entered the main gates of Klugetown, it instantly became clear that this was not the sort of place a pony wanted to find herself alone. The group stuck close to one another, drinking in the strange sights and sounds. Creatures that looked like giant rhinoceroses, beastly pigs and porcupines grunted as they sold mysterious goods from their stalls.

Other townsfolk emerged from shadows to peek and greedily taunt the little candy-coloured equines as they passed by.

"That's a lovely horn … how much?" a cloaked monster whispered to Rarity as she trotted along. Rarity's face contorted in horror at the very thought of such a thing. Across the way, a tower of spiky-beaked birds in cages squawked at Fluttershy as she neared them. The birds were scary-looking, but Fluttershy couldn't imagine what beasts thought it was OK to trap the poor babies!

Twilight searched the perilous streets for a friendly face. Anycreature would do, just as long as they could give any sort of information about where exactly they were right now. Then, Twilight noticed a street vendor struggling to tie barrels of cargo on to his cart. A wayward barrel sprang loose and toppled the entire pile.

"Let me help you with that!" The princess sprang into action, using her magic to catch the barrel in question. But the beast just growled at her to get away from his cart.

"Now, I know we need help, but be careful who you talk to," Twilight warned the others in a low whisper. "And try to blend in!"

But it was too late. Pinkie Pie was already bounding forward into the market square, screaming at the top of her lungs. "CAN ANYPONY TAKE US TO THE QUEEN OF THE HIPPOS?" she shouted. A gigantic blue monster with fish-like fins scoffed in disgust at Pinkie's lack of awareness of the rules.

"You want somethin', you gotta give somethin'!" he grunted.

"Oh!" Pinkie giggled and proceeded to offer the beasts a big hug, a mane comb with a few curly pink hairs woven into it, and a picture of her sister Maud. When they refused all of her offers, Pinkie Pie held out a little white ball. "How about this breath mint?" Pinkie said to the pig monster with stinky breath. "Seriously, buddy. Help me to help you."

Twilight and the others watched on, growing more nervous with each passing minute. This wasn't the sort of place a pony wanted to start teasing anybody. Twilight darted to Pinkie's side and pulled her away from the growling creature. "Pinkie! You can't just take off! And you don't need to announce to every—"

"Relax, Twilight! I've totally got this." Pinkie smiled, waving her hoof nonchalantly. But the two pony friends were so caught up in their conversation that they didn't notice a group of the

scary creatures closing in on them!
Rarity, Applejack and Fluttershy took a
few steps back towards each other. Even
Rainbow Dash looked shaken by the
shouts of the pushy mob.

"How much for the giant gecko?"
yelled one, pointing to Spike.

"Uh …" Twilight
shook her head.
"Spike isn't for sale—"

"I WANT THAT
fancy purple hair!"
shouted another.
"I'll give you TWO
HIPPOS for it!"

"TWO hippos?" Rarity cried out
indignantly. "It's worth more than that."
Unfortunately, this caused the bidding
war for everything the ponies had – and
the ponies themselves – to get louder.

The creatures shouted and argued with one another as they got closer and closer to the ponies.

The friends held on to each other in terror and closed their eyes. Twilight couldn't help but think that this could be the end of their journey, before it had even begun.

Chapter 9
The Friend
That You Need

Luckily, a mysterious fellow named
Capper had been watching the entire
fiasco from the shadows. The lanky,
golden-coloured cat slunk around in his
shabby, deep red trench coat. His
shocking green eyes and the curl of
purple fur on top of his head made him

stand out in a crowd – when he wanted to, that was. And luckily for the little ponies, he decided right now was the perfect time to do so.

"Back up, everyone!" Capper leapt into the middle of the crowd, landing gracefully on his hind legs right in front of the scared ponies. "BACK. IT. UP!" He extended his arms protectively to the greedy crowd of hooligans and spoke directly to them. "Y'all are in some serious danger! You didn't touch any of them, did you?" He pointed to the ponies and feigned concern. It was enough to stop the creatures in their tracks.

"Just look at all those colours – you

think that's natural?" Capper leaned in close and whispered. "They're infected with 'Pastelus Colouritis'!"

The crowd gasped in horror, even though they had no idea what that was. It just sounded quite serious.

Applejack couldn't believe the implication that she and her friends were sick. Why, they were healthy as horses! She stepped forward in a defensive huff. "Now you listen here, fella—"

Capper shot her a look and covered Applejack's mouth with his tail. Then he slyly dipped his tail in some nearby purple liquid and spashed it at the nearest creature. The giant fish man didn't notice. "Don't worry, though—" Capper waltzed and weaved through the crowd in a dizzying movement. "As long as you're not covered in purple splotches, you'll be fine." Capper gasped and pointed at the giant fish man's arms, where the splotches of purple liquid had landed. "Uh oh …"

"What do I do?" he cried out in desperation. The other creatures started to slowly back away from him.

"Enjoy your last moments," Capper smirked. "And don't touch anyone— because parts will fall off."

"Aaaaaahhh!" the crowd screamed, completely forgetting about their pony and dragon prey. Without a second thought, they scrambled to get as far away as possible! Clouds of dust were kicked up in the process and when they settled a moment later, the only souls in the whole vicinity were Capper and the ponies.

"Well, all right …" The smug cat turned back to his new friends to see just how impressed they were with his quick thinking. He grabbed the collar of his red coat and raised his eyebrows expectantly.

"You. Are. AWESOME!" Rainbow Dash flew over, her face breaking out into a look of pure admiration.

"And quite charming ..." Rarity giggled and blushed, oblivious to Spike's jealous grunt.

"Capper's the name," said the cat with a wink. "And charming's my game." He bent down in a deep, formal bow. He locked eyes with Twilight Sparkle. "So, shall I lead you to the hippos then?"

While Pinkie Pie and the others began to follow the cat out of the square, something inside was telling Twilight to be cautious. She held her wing out in front of Pinkie and hissed. "Wait! I don't know if we should trust him ..."

"We could definitely use a friend out here!" Pinkie reminded her. But before Twilight could even consider Pinkie's point, Capper popped up between the two of them.

"You know what?" Capper said, voice as smooth as a purr. "Little Candyfloss Hair is right. This town is not a nice place for little fillies all alone."

"We're not alone," Twilight pointed out. She gestured to her friends. "We have each other."

Capper nodded. "Ah yes, but I know every nook and cranny, every dark twist and corner of this place! You're all actually quite lucky that you ran into me …" His green eyes glowed with mischief.

Applejack cocked her head to the side. "So what're ya sayin' exactly?"

"I'll be the friend you need!" Capper smiled and tugged at his ragged coat. "Follow me and I'll lead you to safety." The cat skipped ahead in a nimble fashion. "And help you find the hippos you seek!"

Finding the Queen of the Hippos was exactly what they did need, so Twilight nodded at the others to go. As they followed Capper, the ponies and Spike all looked to one another for reassurance. Everypony's faces seemed a little unsure, except for Pinkie Pie. But Capper was right – Klugetown was an unfamiliar place and he had saved them from the villagers. What more proof did they need that he was on their side?

Chapter 10

Mind Your Manor

The ponies followed Capper, darting through the darkened streets, past creepy alleyways and tattered curtains. Now and then, Capper scurried ahead and whispered something to a random villager. Whatever he was saying was allowing the group access through secret shortcuts, so the ponies didn't mind the little bit of clandestine activity.

Finally they arrived at a gigantic water mill. Capper hopped on to the wheel and motioned for them to do the same. A moment later, they were whisked up into the belly of the mill tower.

"Welcome, my little ponies, to my little Manor!" Capper announced with pride as they finally entered the strange dwelling. The ponies filed in and Capper got busy at once trying to make them feel comfortable. It wasn't difficult, as his cosy hideaway was full of treasures of all kinds to explore, soft pillows to sit on and refreshments to warm their bellies. It was just what they needed.

"How lovely," cooed Rarity, settling into a purple armchair. She noticed that her mane blended into the colour. It looked fabulous!

"Oh, I feel better already!" Fluttershy said with a satisfied sigh.

Capper pointed to Spike, looking slightly concerned. "Oh, uh, did you housetrain this baby crocodile?"

"Crocodile!" Spike retorted with a  bitter grunt. The little dragon seemed to be the only one in the group unimpressed by Capper. Spike even caught Rarity slyly mooning over an old painting with Capper's face on it.

"So, this Queen of the Hippos – what kind of powers does she have?" Twilight trotted close behind Capper as he fumbled about, fluffing pillows and straightening up. "And how long will it take to get to her?"

"Hippos?" Capper was taken aback.

He grabbed a stack of teacups and began to set the table. "Yeah, they got powers! Heavy, large powers … and, uh … I'll take you soon enough!"

Twilight's eye began to twitch. "We don't have time!"

"Please, please. Relax!" Capper insisted, holding out his paws. "Put your hooves up. There's always time for some dilly-dally tea." He poured a cup for Fluttershy and she took a happy sip.

"Mmmm," she cooed. "This is wonderful."

"I guess we can stay for just a few minutes …" Twilight bit her lip, feeling conflicted. It was nice to see her friends enjoy some rest. The other ponies and Spike didn't have to come with her on this journey and they deserved a few moments to regroup. Even Applejack and

Rainbow Dash sipped their tea gratefully – and they didn't usually like tea!

But that didn't mean Twilight couldn't make good use of this time to learn something from their gracious host. The instant they'd entered Capper's manor, Twilight had noticed the various bookshelves lining the walls. She trotted over to one of them and scanned the titles. Twilight had no idea what she was looking for – a book on hippos? It seemed unlikely that she would find such a perfect answer right in front of her face.

A very old, ornate tome caught her eye. It was a deep maroon colour, with gilded edges and a mysterious map on the cover. It appeared to be an old atlas. Twilight used her magic to gently lift the book from the shelf. But as she did, a loose piece of paper fell out!

"Huh?" Twilight mumbled to herself as she unfolded the discovery. She couldn't help gasping as she laid her eyes on it. It was their key to finding the Queen! The ponies had been looking for the wrong thing this entire time.

CHAPTER 11
Hot Tempered

"Please!" a long-necked vendor cried out as a Storm Creature smashed her booth. "I don't know anything!"

The Storm Creatures tore across the main square of Klugetown with no regard for the destruction they were causing to the vendors' booths. They had strict orders to do anything in their power to find the wretched purple princess pony that had escaped back in Canterlot. Villagers screamed and darted away, frightened by the growls and ferocity that punctuated the massive soldiers' movements.

Tempest trotted behind them, stoically. This trip was a mere inconvenience to her. All she had to do was find that princess and get back to Canterlot. It wouldn't be difficult. That Twilight Sparkle was weak – Tempest just knew it.

"You really think the ponies got this far?" Grubber asked, walking alongside his mistress and munching on an apple tart. He never stopped eating.

Tempest ignored him. Instead she narrowed her eyes and stopped in her tracks. She had noticed a bright pink strand of pony hair caught in a jagged

piece of wooden fence. "Oh, they're here."
This confirmation was all she needed.

"Attention!" Tempest called out, her
voice strong and even. "A purple pony
passed this way. Tell me where she is—"

"Or somethin' real bad's gonna
happen!" Grubber added. The bite of
apple tart he took right after really didn't
do much to make him seem intimidating.

"You think we're gonna fall for this
again?" The giant blue fish man who'd
been told he had 'Pastelus Colouritis'
stepped forward. Obviously, despite what
he'd been told, the beast still had all his
parts. He frowned. "I don't know what
kinda scam you're working with Capper
and the rest of your friends, but—"

Tempest cut him off. "Friends?" She
had assumed the purple pony had been
working alone.

"Poison or no poison ... you're gonna pay!" The angry fish man came at Tempest, thrusting his fishy fist at her muzzle. She snapped into action, ducking his punch and swinging her hoof around. Tempest shot into the air, grabbing his fin by her muzzle. Then she swung the massive beast down to the ground with a giant crash! The fish man groaned in pain.

"Now," the satisfied Unicorn said as she stood over him, her broken horn sparking and sputtering with electric energy. "About this 'Capper' ..." From the scared look on the fish man's face, Tempest knew that she was going to get all the information she needed.

CHAPTER 12
To Settle a Debt

The ponies were all gathered around Capper, sharing stories from Equestria. Rainbow Dash was deep into her story about the first time she'd ever successfully performed a Sonic Rainboom – the most epic stunt a Pegasus could attempt – when Rarity trotted over to fix Capper's coat. She'd found some spare thread used her magic to make a few expert stitches.

"Here you go!" Rarity said as she finished up. "I do apologise. If we were back home, I could have matched the coat from your portrait." The unicorn gestured her hoof to the painting on the wall.

"Whoa." Capper's jaw dropped when he caught his reflection in the mirror. He couldn't believe how much better his coat looked. It was almost like new! But why was Rarity helping him with this? Capper stroked his whiskers and raised his eyebrow. "OK, what's the catch?"

"Nothing! After all you've done for us?" Rarity smiled warmly. "Consider it a thank you."

"Oh, don't thank me. Really ..." A wave of guilt washed over Capper. What had he done to these poor ponies that now considered him friends? He deflated with the weight of his secret. Capper opened his mouth and was considering telling them the truth about why he was being so hospitable when Twilight Sparkle came rushing into the room.

"We've been looking for the wrong queen!" Twilight exclaimed. She unfurled a scroll and laid it on the table. It was a map! The ponies all gathered around to look. Twilight pointed at an illustration. "We don't need the Queen of the Hippos – we need the Queen of the Hippogriffs! They're part pony, part eagle."

The ponies all turned to Capper for any insight on the development. It didn't really add up. Capper scrambled to come up with something. "Oh! The HippoGRIFFS? Now the trouble with that is, no one knows where they are ..."

Twilight frowned, suspicious. "It says

right here that they're on the top of Mount Aris."

"Oooh!" Pinkie Pie pointed her hoof at the window. "You mean the mountain right outside?" Sure enough, far off in the distance was a tall peak, surrounded by clouds that looked almost identical to the one in the map illustration.

Twilight couldn't believe Capper had withheld such important information from them, when he'd clearly known about the Hippogriffs all along. She shot him a disappointed look, folded her map and turned to her friends. "Let's go, everypony."

"Wait!" The cat sprang to the doorway in a panic, blocking the ponies' way. "You can't make it there by yourselves! You need an airship – and lucky for you, I can get you a ride!"

Twilight narrowed her eyes and pushed past him. "I think we can get there on our own …"

But when she opened the door, a giant mole rat in a raggedy suit and top hat stood waiting outside! He smiled, exposing his sickly yellow teeth.

"Here's Verko!" he laughed with sneaky satisfaction. He leaned past Twilight and met Capper's eyes. "These

ponies better shoot rainbow lasers outta their eyes if they're going to settle your debt, Capper!" He gestured to a gigantic cage on wheels behind him. "Let's load 'em up!"

The ponies gasped.

Capper was planning to sell them? Applejack shook her head in disappointment and Rarity had to fan herself with her hoof to get over the shock of it all. What a double-crossing, good-for-nothing feline scoundrel! All Capper did in reply was tug on his jacket collar and laugh nervously. That pretty much confirmed his guilt.

Verko scampered in, his little mole rat feet scratching against the floor. He had just begun to size the ponies up when a faint sparking sound came from outside. *Clip, clop. Clip, clop.* The sound of hooves followed and a shadowy figure appeared in the outline of the doorway.

"Silly little ponies …"

"Tempest!" Twilight gasped. Her worst fears were starting to come true! She and her friends were going to be captured and they would never be able to save Equestria. Everypony was visibly shaken. Fluttershy cowered behind the others.

"Trusting strangers, I see?" Tempest sized up Capper and trotted in, raising a confident eyebrow. "Big mistake. Big."

"Huge!" Grubber added, following his master.

Verko, the salesmole, scrambled over to the tiny new guests. Maybe he could make a bit or two off this strange pony, too! He took Tempest's cheeks in his little claws and squashed them around. "Scary broken horn! What tricks do you know, my little pony-wony?"

Tempest was getting angrier by the second. Her horn sparked menacingly.

Tempest sent a shock of lightning across the room at Verko! They were both distracted – it was now or never. "Go, go!"

Twilight whispered as she opened the window with her magic. The ponies sprang into action. They were all out of the window before Verko had even hit the floor from Tempest's stun magic.

When Tempest saw Twilight flying out the window, she began to sizzle with rage. "Get her – now!" she called out to her Storm Creatures, stomping her hoof on the ground.

Tempest didn't understand what was happening. How could that little princess have escaped her grasp a second time? Tempest had underestimated the purple pony, but one thing was certain … Twilight Sparkle wouldn't escape again. Tempest and the Storm King would make sure of that.

Chapter 13
Best Escape Plan Ever

"Aaaaaahhh!" the ponies screamed as they barrelled through Klugetown. Who could have predicted the giant wooden windmill wheel would come loose when they'd all jumped on it outside Capper's manor? They clutched the surface tightly with their hooves as Rainbow Dash and

Twilight tried to steer the makeshift craft out of harm's way. It was no use!

The Storm Creatures were hot on their hooves as the wheel rolled through streets and buildings, shattering everything in its path. Somepony had to stop this thing. "Jump!" Applejack cried out as soon as she spotted a jagged, elevated walkway. The ponies leapt on to the wooden planks and galloped across, the wheel now careening towards them!

"We have to get there!" Twilight Sparkled shouted and pointed her hoof directly ahead of them. "To the docks!" Several walkways jutted out from the side of tall buildings. Anchored to the highest port of one was a massive floating ship! It definitely wasn't one of the Storm King's fleet.

But it was in the process of leaving!

"Hurry!" Twilight urged as she soared behind her friends to make sure they were all safe. The ponies' manes billowed out behind them as they galloped as fast as their hooves would carry them on to the airship.

Rainbow Dash, in a moment of quick thinking, flew ahead and grabbed the mooring rope with her teeth. She pulled it taut enough for Rarity, Applejack and Spike to carefully tightrope-walk across it. Fluttershy flew above, encouraging them. "That's it! Don't look down now."

"YAY!" squealed Pinkie Pie as she took an enthusiastic bounce on to the rope.

The jump caused the rope to buckle. Spike began to lose his footing and disaster struck! Spike and Rainbow both managed to grab hold of the rope, but Pinkie Pie wasn't so lucky. The pink pony wailed in despair as she plummeted down, heading right in the direction of some very craggy-looking rocks!

"Pinkie!" Twilight cried out as she darted to Pinkie's rescue. She reached her friend with just a second to spare and carried her back up to safety, putting her on the deck of the ship with the others.

Almost immediately, Pinkie popped up and thrust her hoof into the air. "Best. Escape plan. EVER!!!" Twilight was going to protest this statement, but suddenly she and Pinkie found themselves lassoed and dragged away. Applejack had pulled them behind some boxes on the deck.

"Shhhh!" Rarity whispered.

"Hey, did you hear somethin'?" one big shadowy figure said to his buddy, who just squawked in reply. From their outlines, they looked like large … birds? Perhaps they were Griffon sailors! Twilight felt a twinge of hope. She knew the Griffon Kingdom – maybe these Griffon strangers would know some of her friends and help deliver her to Mount Aris as an act of goodwill and friendship to Equestria. What a stroke of luck landing on this ship had been!

They were already heading in the right direction. It should be no problem finding the Queen of the Hippogriffs. After they got her help, all of this would be over soon. Twilight could just feel it.

✶ ✶ ✶

"OK!" Capper wailed as the Storm Creatures threw his body on to the dock by Tempest's airship. Being taken prisoner by the Storm Guard was not something that had been in his plans today. "No need for violence! The ponies are headed to …" Capper almost told the truth, but then hesitated, thinking of how the kind ponies had mended his coat and called him 'friend'. They didn't deserve to be given up so easily again.

Tempest loomed over him, tapping her hoof impatiently. "Well?"

"They're headed east! Yeah … to Black Skull Island." Capper nodded with his signature cool-cat confidence.

"So glad I could be of service! I'll just be on my way—"

Tempest stepped in front of Capper, blocking his path back home. "When I get my princess. Until then, your fate is still … up in the air." Capper's face fell. This couldn't be happening.

"Ohhh! You're our prisoner!" Grubber laughed in delight. "We're going in a skiff. Which is a boat, specifically an airboat." The squat creature motioned to the warriors. Once their captor was tied up and safe inside, Tempest took the helm. Time was running out before the Storm King's arrival.

And Tempest could not afford to fail him.

CHAPTER 14
The Rulebook

As the airship soared through the misty clouds, Twilight studied the map she'd borrowed from Capper's place. Judging by the landmarks in the illustration, Twilight was fairly confident they were heading in the direction of Mount Aris, but they needed to be sure. There was only one way to find out where this ship was actually going. They were going to have to talk to someone.

Applejack and Rainbow Dash peered out from behind the wooden crate to assess their situation. The crew members of the airship looked kind of like giant birds – but they definitely weren't Griffons. They wore black uniforms and had grumpy expressions on their faces as they waddled back and forth across the deck with their boxes of mysterious cargo.

"What do ya think, Twilight?" Applejack asked. "Should we just … ask 'em to take us?"

Twilight bit her lip, unsure. "The last time we trusted somepony, he tried to sell us!" The other ponies nodded, considering this. None of them could quite believe they'd almost been caged and sold as goods.

Suddenly, their hiding place started to shift. A box was lifted and the ponies

were exposed!
Staring
straight
back at
them was a
gigantic
green parrot
with a scowl
on his face.

"Hey, Captain Celaeno!" shouted one
of the birds. "We supposed to be shipping
livestock today?"

A white-feathered bird with a crystal
peg leg hobbled forward and sighed. "No,
Boyle ... looks like we have stowaways."
She appeared to be more inconvenienced
by the discovery than upset.

"What do we do now?" Boyle and
Captain Celaeno looked to one another
for an answer, but both came up short.

The latter whipped out a huge book and began to leaf through it. She had clearly been through this routine before.

"The Storm King's rulebook says ..." Captain Celaeno read aloud. She turned to the rest of her parrot crew and shouted. "THROW 'EM OVERBOARD!"

Overboard? Twilight and her friends huddled together in fear. Fluttershy kept her eyes shut and whimpered as the parrots closed in. With each step closer, the ponies felt more hopeless. They were doomed ...

FWEEEEEE! Just then a whistle sounded. At the sound of the noise, every crewmember stopped what they were doing and began to trudge away. "All right, that's lunch!" Captain Celaeno sighed. "C'mon everybody, we get fifteen minutes! Scarf it down."

At the mere mention of food, Rainbow Dash's tummy began to rumble. It had been for ever since the ponies had last eaten a meal and seeing as they were obviously not getting thrown overboard, she saw an opportunity. "Uh ... can we have some food?"

"Food ... food ..." Captain Celaeno consulted her rulebook. She slammed it shut and shrugged. "Eh, nothing here says you can't." The ponies cheered with excitement. Their fate had changed so quickly!

"Oh, thank goodness!" said Rarity, sighing with relief and silently wondering if the parrots usually had tea to go with the lunch. How delightful this was going to be!

But once seated at the long table in the mess hall, the ponies were presented with big slops of gruel. No sandwiches, no fresh apples and certainly not a single drop of tea! "Oh, what a shame," Rarity laughed uncomfortably, sizing up her portion of gruel. "I just ate … several days ago!"

The birds calmly tucked into their food, seemingly having forgotten all about the stowaway thing. Everyone was distracted. Actually, there was something strange about this whole ship.

"So, you were about to toss us overboard …" Rainbow Dash said through a mouthful of gruel. She ignored the panicked look from Twilight. "... And you stopped for a lunch break?"

Boyle, the green parrot who had discovered the ponies, put his fork down and slumped sadly. "The Storm King only allows us one break a day for meals. Then it's back to hauling goods."

Spike perked up. "So you're just delivery guys?"

"And gals," Captain Celaeno said, tugging on her unflattering uniform emblazoned with the Storm King's insignia. "These aren't exactly doing us any favours."

This was perfect, Twilight realised. If they were delivery birds, then certainly they could help out. What difference were a few little ponies instead of some cargo in the grand scheme of things?

"Then, can you deliver us to Mount Aris?" she said with a friendly smile.

"Sorry," Captain Celaeno shook her head. "We do what the Storm King orders. Or we suffer his wrath." She went back to eating her food sadly.

A moment of silence passed. "But what did you guys do before the Storm King?" Rainbow Dash pried. She knew that there was more to this story and she wasn't giving up that easily. "What's that?" She pointed her hoof at a flag that had been covered up by a poster of the Storm King.

Mullet, the first mate bird, pulled the poster back. Underneath was a black flag bearing a skull and crossbones! Rainbow Dash gasped. She knew what that meant. "Whoa! You used to be pirates!"

Chapter 15
Time to be Awesome

The birds all looked at one another sheepishly. "We prefered the term 'Swashbuckling Treasure Hunters'," Mullet said with a sly smirk. He looked off into the distance, like he was happily remembering his swashbuckling days.

"So … pirates." Rainbow smiled in satisfaction. She sprang to her hooves and looked Captain Celaeno in her sad eyes. "The way I see it – you birds have a choice to make."

"We do?" The birds were intrigued.

"What do you mean?" Boyle grunted.

Rainbow flew over to the poster and gestured to it. "You can let some hoity-toity Storm King tell you how to live your lives or …" She ripped the poster down, letting the pirate flag fly free. "… You can be awesome again!"

A murmur of whispers broke out amongst the bird shipmates. At first, Twilight was nervous Rainbow Dash had offended their unlikely hosts, but it was quite the opposite. For the first time since the ponies had arrived on Captain Celaeno's ship, the birds were smiling!

"The little rainbow pony is right," Captain Celaeno agreed as she stood up.

"It's time to be awesome!" She puffed her chest out with pride. "Come on, scallywags! Let's show these little ponies how it's done!" The parrots cheered and followed orders, marching out to the deck with their leader.

"Yeahhh!" Pinkie Pie cheered, bounding after them. The other ponies trotted out as well, grinning from ear to ear.

The birds got to work restoring their ship to its former, swashbuckling glory. They all sang and whistled as decks were swabbed, flags were flown and chests of gems were unlocked and admired.

Back at the helm of her ship, Captain Celaeno placed a huge pirate hat on her head. It had a huge pink feather in it. She stood proudly, a mischievous smile upon her beak.

"Awesome!" Rainbow Dash cheered, zipping underneath the sails and past the pirate crew. "And now for the finishing touch!"

"Rainboom, rainboom, rainboom!" Pinkie Pie started the chant. It wasn't long before the other ponies and birds started chanting and clapping along in encouragement, too. All except Twilight, who suddenly realised the implications of a gigantic signal showing their whereabouts. "No no no no no … NO!" she cried out.

But it was too late. Rainbow Dash was already soaring into the sky with a huge smile on her face. Once she was far enough away she looped around and dived down at top speed. The Pegasus looped around the airship, creating a rainbow spiral around the pirates.

Everyone watched in delighted wonder as the colourful pattern burst from every direction in a beautiful explosion. Captain Celaeno and her crew had never seen anything so spectacular before.

"Aw yeah!" Rainbow Dash laughed. There was nothing more exhilarating than performing a Sonic Rainboom, especially after being cooped up for so long. "Woooo!" she shouted with unfettered glee.

Across the sky, Tempest was also experiencing something close to happiness. Because the pretty picture in the sky was as good as a map to finding those little ponies.

"Change course from Black Skull Island to …" Tempest narrowed her eyes at Capper and pointed in the direction of the rainbow blast. "… That way." Grubber put down his piece of cake, nodded and motioned to the beasts. But he was going too slowly for Tempest. She pushed him aside and spun the steering wheel herself. The entire ship lurched and Tempest gave a wicked laugh. She hoped the ponies were having a good time, because it would be their last.

CHAPTER 16
The Changing Tide

When the dark clouds began to roll in,
Captain Celaeno sounded the alarm
immediately. What was happening?
Rainbow Dash and the other ponies
looked to their new comrades for answers.

"Storm Creatures!" Captain Celaeno
squawked. "It looks like they've tracked
you down!"

Twilight's face contorted into anguish. "Tempest!"

"Secure the rigging! Lock down the cargo!" Captain Celaeno ordered. "Everyone – prepare for lockdown! They can't take these ponies!"

Applejack's eyes were as wide as apples. "Oh no!"

"Goodness!" Fluttershy whispered.

Boyle led Applejack, Pinkie Pie, Fluttershy, Rarity and Rainbow Dash to a trap door. They galloped inside to hide. Luckily, the transfixed Twilight slipped in at the very last moment. As the hatch shut, the ponies held their breath anxiously.

Rainbow Dash finally broke the silence. "You … think she saw my Rainboom?" Her cheeks blushed pink with embarrassment. She had just been trying to liven up the party, not ruin their whole adventure!

"Are you KIDDING me?" Twilight retorted. She began to pace back and forth, which was never a good sign. "This is bad. This is bad. This is VERY bad!"

Suddenly, the airship lurched as a harpoon above deck made contact and began to reel them in to the skiff. "Ahhh!" the ponies shouted as they all fell into a pile. They craned to listen as Tempest and the Storm Creatures boarded the craft. A long series of murmurs followed.

"What are they saying?" Pinkie Pie whispered. "Nice things?"

"They're asking where I am!" Twilight exclaimed. She was already a ball of nerves. "Tempest is accusing them of sheltering fugitives and threatening them

with the wrath of the Storm King …"
Twilight began to panic. "We have to get off this ship before they tell Tempest we're here!"

Rainbow Dash scoffed. "We helped them get their mojo back. They're not going to give us up!" Rarity and Applejack nodded in agreement, but it did nothing to calm Twilight. She was getting that twitchy look she sometimes had when she was trying to impress the other princesses. But all they could do was keep quiet and wait it out.

Up above, Tempest had had enough. She'd pointed out Captain Celaeno and her crew's silly outfits. They were supposed to be wearing standard-issue Storm King brand delivery gear. Celaeno had claimed they were just having a pirate-themed party. It was very fishy.

The rulebook didn't allow time for parties, so they were definitely lying.

"You know who else is really good at parties?" Tempest growled. "Ponies. Now, I'm gonna count to three, and if you don't tell me where they are, your ship is going down!" But before she could even count, Tempest was interrupted by a loud shriek. She galloped over to the underbelly. One glance confirmed it – the trapdoor in the bottom of the airship was open. The ponies must have used it to escape!

Tempest scanned the sky for the colourful equines but couldn't see anything. Tempest stomped her hoof on the deck in frustration. She peered over the edge one last time, hoping that the ponies had all made it out alive. Not because she cared much, but because Tempest wanted that princess in one piece. And she would get her.

"Hey, Tempest!" Grubber shouted. He ambled up, holding a cupcake and a worn piece of scroll.

"What's that?" she barked. Couldn't he see she was busy trying to wallow in her own frustration right now?

"I found this. It's a kind of cupcake thing with sprinkles ..." Grubber grinned. "And this is ... uh ..."

Tempest yanked the scroll from his claw and unfurled it. There were crazy-looking scribbles all over it. "It's a map," Tempest observed. And it was the perfect clue. "They're going to Mount Aris."

Chapter 17
To Mount Aris

"Heeyew!" Applejack sighed with relief. She placed her hooves on the edge of the wooden box that had become their makeshift hot-air balloon basket and peered out at the landscape of bushy green trees below. "That was some quick thinkin', Twilight!"

"Yes, darling!" Rarity marvelled. "How

in the world did you gather all of those items and assemble them in mid-air while we were plummeting to our doom?" She smoothed her mane down. "And using Spike's fire-breathing abilities to heat the balloon? Truly inspired." Spike beamed at the compliment.

"Next stop, Mount Aris!" Rainbow Dash called out as she flew alongside the hot-air balloon. She pointed to the narrow, pointy mountain in the distance.

"I don't know how I did it," Twilight admitted. "But it was great. And now we're on our way to Mount Aris!" She took a deep breath. The air somehow seemed sweeter on the heels of victory. "Yahooo!"

* * *

The stone stairs to Mount Aris were winding and endless. As they trudged upwards, the ponies were reaching a new level of exhausted. It didn't help that the landscape was completely desolate, either. It was pretty depressing.

Rarity, in particular, was beginning to get quite whiny. "That's it! I simply. Cannot. Even! I have nothing. The bad guys have won!" She collapsed into a dramatic heap on the ground. "I'm so sorry ..."

Rainbow Dash, who had been periodically flying above to check their progress, called down some words of encouragement. "We're almost there!"

"Will you stop saying that?" Rarity huffed. Instances such as these were the only times she was truly jealous of Rainbow for having wings.

Rainbow brightened. "No, really –
we're here!"

It was the final push they all needed.
The ponies sped up, taking the last sets of
stairs twice as fast. When they finally
reached the top and saw the entrance, it
all felt worth the journey. "This is it!"
Twilight exclaimed. Excitement bubbled
up inside her stomach.

They all stood back and admired the
sight. Mount Aris was eerie and beautiful.
Two stone columns carved into the shape
of ancient Hippogriffs flanked a walkway,
inviting visitors in with a sense of mystery
and mysticism. Twilight, a history buff,
felt a twinge of intrigue that made her
want to read everything ever written
about these creatures. She could recall
learning next to nothing about them in
her studies.

"Well, I'll be …!" marvelled Applejack, leaning back so far that her brown hat almost fell clean off her head. Once she'd secured it back on her head, she trotted in through the gates behind the others.

"Are we sure this is the right place?" asked Rarity, looking around the deserted street. It did look a little the worse for wear, with all of the cracked statues and toppled pillars everywhere. Many of the beautiful domed  dwellings had their doors left ajar, and weeds had begun to grow everywhere.

"Hello?" Applejack called out. "Is anypony home?"

Pinkie Pie bounced around, looking for signs of life. "No hippogriffies here.

Or here. Or here! Wait …" Pinkie crouched down and lifted a little rock with her muzzle. "Nope. This place is emp-ty!"

Empty? After everything the ponies had gone through to get to Mount Aris, Twilight didn't understand. Celestia believed that the only way to save Equestria was to find the Queen of the Hippogriffs, or she wouldn't have instructed Luna to go and find her.

"Well, where are they?" Twilight said in disbelief.

Spike scanned the desolate landscape and shuddered. "Something bad happened here. Something turned this whole place into a ghost town!"

"A g-g-ghost town?" Fluttershy whimpered. She didn't like the idea of ghosts, or anything remotely scary.

Getting ready for the Friendship Festival

Princess Twilight meets Songbird Serenade

Tempest Shadow turns the princesses to stone!

The ponies escape down a waterfall

Meeting Capper

Meeting Captain Celaeno and her crew

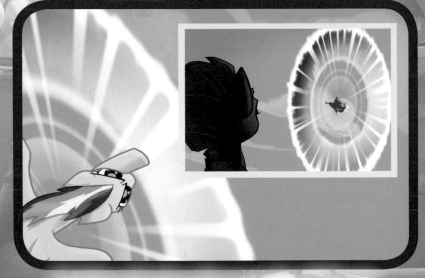

Rainbow Dash makes a sonic rainboom

The ponies are swept into a vortex

Meeting the Seaponies!

Princess Twilight Sparkle is captured

A plan to free Twilight

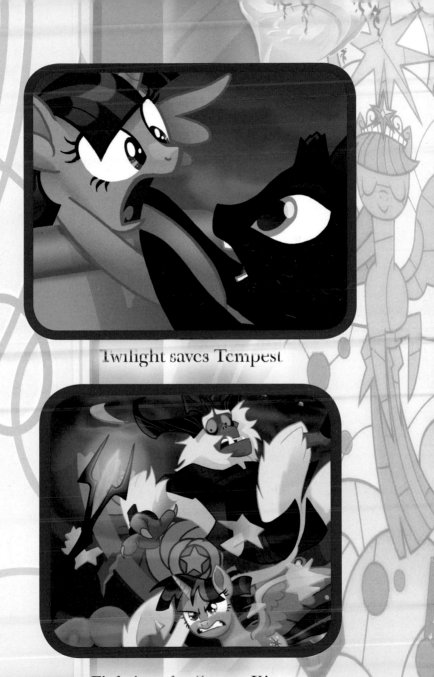

Twilight saves Tempest

Fighting the Storm King

The spell on the princesses is broken

Happy Friendship Festival!

"Wait!" Rarity perked up and began to look around. "What's that gorgeous sound? It's like a song …" The ponies listened closely. There was a beautiful voice echoing through the empty city. *Aaaaaah … ahhhhh … ahhhhh!* The melody was familiar and haunting at the same time. The ponies bravely trotted along, searching for the source.

"It's coming from over there!" In the distance, Twilight noticed an interesting building with tall archways. Like everything else there, it had been partially destroyed, but it looked as if it had once been a magnificent cathedral.

Inside, the singing grew even louder. The sound was amplified by the acoustics of the cavernous space. *Ahhhh … ahhhh …* The pretty melody continued, but was now accompanied by the splish-splash of

running water, for there was a large
fountain in the centre of the room. It was
set in the middle of a small pond and
shaped like a pink lotus flower, just like
the kind the ponies used in treatments
back at the Ponyville Day Spa.

Was that a shadow of somepony
behind the flower? It was too murky to see
the fountain properly. Rarity stepped
forward for a closer look and couldn't
help gasping at its sheer beauty. A few
rocks underhoof tumbled down and
plopped into the water.

"What was that?" The shadowy figure
gasped and leapt into the water, causing a
splash of water to spray on to the ponies.

Twilight and Rarity exchanged an
excited look. The hippogriffs might have
been long gone, but there was definitely
somepony here. Maybe this mystery

creature could help them find the queen!

"Hey! Wait up!" Pinkie Pie called out. She leapt without any hesitation right into the water. "CANNONBALL!"

"Pinkie!" Twilight cried out and jumped in after her. One by one, the other ponies and Spike jumped in, too. *SPLASH!* But the creature was gone. Pinkie's mane dripped, sad and wet against her face. Applejack was about to console her friend when the pond started to swirl, pulling them into a whirlpool!

"AAAAAHHH!" they all screamed.

The ponies were being sucked underwater and there was no way to escape!

Chapter 18
The Depths of Despair

Everything was dark. Twilight moved her hooves around, reaching for anything to grab on to, but all she felt was the sensation of being submerged in deep water. She was still holding her breath and desperately needed air. Twilight wanted to magically get some but everything felt fuzzy and she couldn't remember how to use her horn until …

POP! A bubble appeared around Twilight's head. She exhaled gratefully and lit up her horn. All of her friends were wearing bubbles, too! They looked just as relieved as she did.

"Way to leave it till the last minute, Twilight!" Pinkie Pie joked, poking at the bubble's sturdy surface with her hoof.

Twilight shook her head, incredulous. "I didn't make these bubbles …"

"Then …" Fluttershy's eyes grew wide with a mixture of fear and wonder. "Who did?" She swam closer to the other ponies and they formed an underwater huddle.

Suddenly, something swam past! It was impossible to tell what, but it looked like the outline of a fish. Twilight really hoped it wasn't a shark. "Hello?" she called. "We're looking for the Hippogriffs …"

A glowing yellow orb shot towards the ponies, lighting up the whole area. It was so bright and mesmerising. "How do I know I can trust you?" it said.

"Please!" Twilight begged. "The Storm King invaded our land and we need to find the Hippogriffs—"

"The Storm King?" The orb glowed even brighter as it came closer, transforming into something incredible. Twilight had never thought they were real, but swimming right before them was definitely a Seapony! She had pale yellow scales, aqua-coloured fins instead of a mane, pink fluttery wings and a beautiful fish tail instead of back hooves.

"I'm so glad I saved you guys!" she squealed in her cute voice. She sounded even more chipper than Pinkie Pie after eating cupcakes. "I'm Princess Skystar. I'm totally taking you guys to my mum!"

Princess Skystar grabbed Twilight's hoof. The ponies formed a chain and let her lead them down into the watery unknown. They swam past rocks and schools of colourful fishes, into a sea cave tunnel, and beyond. "We're almost there!" Skystar assured them. She giggled in excited anticipation as she swam through a rocky opening and into a glowing underwater paradise.

"This is where I live!" Skystar held out her hoof to present the place to the ponies with pride. Happy Seapony families swam around the sparkling wonderland, giving the princess little nods as she passed by and wondering about the strangers she was escorting. Just up ahead, a palace in the shape of an upside-down flower opened to receive Skystar and the guests.

"Wow!" Spike marvelled, spinning upside down in the water. Rainbow Dash helped to turn him upright again.

"I know! I know!" Skystar giggled happily. Her visitors had barely seen anything yet and they were already impressed. Once they'd swum up into the flower palace, Skystar approached a pearly white seapony with purple fins lounging luxuriously on a purple throne. She wore a golden crown. Skystar swam up to her. "Mother! Look what I found!"

"Is it another shell? Because I am telling you, if it is another shell I am—" Queen Novo replied without looking up.

When she finally did notice Twilight and the others, she let out a massive gasp. "Princess Skystar! What have you done? You know surface dwellers are forbidden here!" At this, several royal guards sprang to action, surrounding the ponies with sharp-looking spears.

"No, no, no, no, Mum, Mum, Mum, Mum, PLEASE!" Princess Skystar whined. "It is SO not like that! The Storm King is trying to destroy their home, too."

"We need to find the Hippogriffs," Twilight called out bravely. The guard pointing a spear at her narrowed his eyes, but Twilight ignored him. This was important. "Do you know what happened to them?"

Queen Novo sighed. "Well, of course I know. I'm the queen. I know everything."

"Oooh! Oooh!" Princess Skystar

smiled wide and clasped her finned hooves together in unabashed delight. "It is such a good story!"

But Queen Novo was holding back for some reason. "Don't you dare tell them!" she chided her daughter and the two began to bicker playfully. Finally, Skystar ignored her mother's wishes and swam up to the wall of the palace.

"Once upon a time, like … a while ago, the Hippogriffs did live on Mount Aris!" Skystar touched the wall with her hoof and it magically began to light up with a glowing illustration of the Hippogriffs and the Storm King. "But that horned beast showed up to steal their magic!"

Twilight met the worried eyes of Applejack and Rainbow Dash. They were all nervous about hearing the next part. Even Spike was biting his lip. What if

Skystar said that the Storm King had destroyed the Hippogriffs entirely? What would that mean for Equestria? The bubbles on their heads allowed them to breathe, but they all held their breath in nervous anticipation.

"But …" Skystar smiled brightly. "To keep their kingdom out of his clutches, their brave and majestic leader, Queen Novo, hid them deep underwater where he could never go." The wall glowed with a scene depicting the same beautiful seapony kingdom in which they were now floating! "We are … well, we *were*, the Hippogriffs!" Skystar gestured to the palace and the seaponies around them. She let out a jovial giggle. "TA DAH!"

"Well, I guess the pearl is out of the oyster now." Queen Novo sighed. "I am the Queen of the Hippogriffs."

Twilight found herself grinning with delight. They had really found her – the Queen of the Hippogriffs was right in front of them! She didn't seem overly accommodating, but Skystar seemed to like Twilight and her friends. She would definitely help save Equestria!

"Hold on now, let me get this straight." Applejack cocked her head to the side. "When the Storm King came, you just abandoned your entire city and fled?"

Skystar smiled and rolled her eyes. "We didn't flee! We swam … you know, in order to flee!"

"But how?" asked Rainbow Dash. Ponies didn't randomly transform into other species, so she couldn't imagine how the Hippogriffs had managed it.

"Oh!" Princess Skystar swam over to her mother. She began to flip her tail and twirl around excitedly. "Can we show them? These are the first guests we've had in, like, FOR EVER! Can we, can we?"

Queen Novo raised an eyebrow and sized up the ponies again. She still wasn't sure if it was a good idea that they were here or not, but the damage had already been done. "Well, I suppose I should make sure it still works," she said, swimming up to the giant jellyfish above her throne. Novo gave it a gentle tap and immediately, the tendrils parted to reveal a glittering, luminescent pink pearl.

It glowed so brightly that its light touched the entire palace. Magic began to swirl around, reaching for Spike and the ponies. Before they realised what was happening, their bubble helmets had disappeared and they had been transformed into seaponies as well!

"These fins are divine!" gushed Rarity, admiring her pretty new tail. The purple fins were curled perfectly, just like her mane had been.

Rainbow Dash sped around in a circle with expert form. Swimming was entirely different from flying, but it was just as awesome. She zoomed back to her friends. "Hey, Applejack! I'll race you to that coral!"

"You're on!" Applejack called back, and the two of them zipped away.

"Woohoo!" Pinkie Pie laughed, doing twirls and blowing bubbles. "Try it, Fluttershy!"

"Yay," Fluttershy said, barely moving her tail.

"Guys," Spike said in confusion. "Guys! What is happening?" The poor dragon had become a puffer fish! He ballooned out and began to float upwards. Everypony giggled.

Twilight observed her friends with elation. She swam up to Novo and Skystar and "This is amazing! With this, we could transform everypony at home into something POWERFUL enough to face the Storm King's army!"

Queen Novo's face grew dark. "Or it could end up in his greedy claws …" She swam back her to beloved treasure and plucked it away.

Novo didn't like how sad it made the young purple pony to see her take the pearl away and hide it back with the jellyfish, but she knew what she had to do. "Honey, I'm sorry about your home. I truly am. But my responsibility is to protect my subjects. The pearl is not going anywhere."

But they had come all this way. Queen Novo and the Hippogriffs couldn't just hide down here for ever. There was so much they were missing up on land! As the queen bade them farewell and left for her afternoon seaweed wrap, Twilight could only keep one thing on her mind – that pearl. She was going to borrow it. Hopefully before anypony found out …

CHAPTER 19
One Small Thing

Princess Skystar was quite apologetic about her mother's behaviour. She explained that it had been such a long time since her mother, or any Seapony for that matter, had interacted with outsiders. They had grown wary of anypony that wasn't with them, because they might be against them. And even though their ordeal with the Storm King had been a long time ago, they were still very afraid of his wrath.

"So that's it," said Applejack, feeling defeated. "You can't help us? We left home for nothin'?"

"No …" Princess Skystar brightened. "Ohmigosh, I have the best idea – you can stay with us … FOR EVER!" She swam back and forth, her pretty aqua fins shaking with excited fervour. "There are so many things we can do! We could make friendship bracelets out of shells, and picture frames out of shells, and decorative wastebaskets out of shells. Oh, it's so wonderful to have new friends to share my shells with!"

"Oh …" Rarity said gently.

She hated to shoot down the hopeful look in Skystar's eyes after she had been so wonderful to them. "That sounds lovely, darling, but you must realise we can't stay."

The Seapony princess slumped in sadness. "Oh no. Of course. Of course! Of course you have your own friends back home. It's fine – it's fine!" She turned around to go, completely deflated. "It's probably for the best. Yeah, I'll just, um, I'll get Mum to, uh, turn you back so you can go home."

Pinkie Pie felt just awful. The thing that she hated more than anything in world – or the sea – was seeing somepony be so gloomy. "I know we have to go, but you guys saw how disappointed Princess Skystar was. Couldn't we stay for just a little longer?"

Applejack was about to protest when Twilight surprised everypony. "Pinkie's right," Twilight said with a nod. "We do have time to do one small thing with Skystar!" Twilight's eyes darted around.

"Say what now?" Rainbow Dash asked, suspicious.

"Well, we still need to come up with a plan to get back. A few minutes won't make a huge difference. And if there's anypony who can cram a lifetime of fun into the blink of an eye, it's Pinkie Pie. So go ahead and show Skystar the best time ever!" Twilight chirped. She threw up her hooves and gestured for them all to go. "I'll catch up with you."

Once they'd swum off to entertain Princess Skystar, Twilight was finally alone with the jellyfish. She looked around to make sure she was by herself.

Luckily, the Seapony guards had followed Queen Novo to her appointment. It was Twilight's only chance to do something sneaky. She was going to steal the Pearl of Transformation!

"Come on," Twilight mumbled to herself and approached the jellyfish just as Queen Novo had. She reached out her hoof and gently tapped on one of the tentacles. But instead of parting to reveal the pearl for taking, the tentacles reached for Twilight and curled around her hooves! She was trapped. The more she struggled against their grasp, the tighter they wound themselves around her. "Ahhh!" Twilight screamed. She hadn't meant to cause a commotion but it was too late.

Within seconds, the Seapony guards returned to find the thief tangled in the scene. They looked furious, but not as angry as Queen Novo, who swam up after them. "All of this so you could sneak in and take the pearl? See, Skystar? This is why we don't bring strangers home!"

Applejack, Rainbow Dash, Rarity, Pinkie Pie, Fluttershy and Spike hung back behind Princess Skystar. She looked so hurt and betrayed. Twilight felt awful for causing Skystar and the Seaponies distress, but she was still determined to get the one thing that would save the ponies of Equestria. Twilight reached out one last time …

FLASH! A blast of white light blinded her.

The next thing Twilight saw was the shore at the foot of Mount Aris.

CHAPTER 20
Friends Like You

The bedraggled ponies rubbed the water out of their eyes as they peeled themselves from the ground. Once they were back on their hooves, they wasted no time. Applejack marched right up to Twilight and stomped her hoof in the sand. "What were you thinking, Twilight? I mean, stealing their pearl?"

"It was the only way to save Equestria!" Twilight explained.

"Except it WASN'T!" Pinkie Pie said, her bottom lip jutting out in a pink pout. "The queen was going to say yes! We showed Skystar friendship and that's what made her realise we were ponies worth saving." She began to pace around, thinking. She stopped dead in her tracks, coming to a realisation. "Unless … you didn't really want us to show Skystar the best time ever! You just wanted us to distract her!"

Everypony stared at Twilight in horror. Was it true?

Twilight let out a growl. "I never would have done it, but this isn't Equestria!

We can't just dance around with con artists, make rainbooms in the sky and expect everything to work out! It's NOT enough. WE are NOT enough!"

Pinkie Pie shook her pink mane sadly. "No, Twilight. We were gonna get the help we needed. The only thing that stopped us was you."

This was ridiculous. Why couldn't Twilight's friends see that she was doing the best she could? The pressure of this entire situation was all on Twilight Sparkle. She was the one who Tempest was after and she was the last Princess of Equestria. "I'm the only one they want!" she said.

"You're also the only one who doesn't trust her friends!" Pinkie Pie retorted. The other ponies nodded in agreement.

That was enough. Twilight looked up

to the spiky, desolate Mount Aris and something snapped inside her. This was all too much. Her friends had been nothing but trouble for her. She spun around on her hoof and narrowed her eyes. "Well, maybe I would have been better off without FRIENDS LIKE YOU!" Twilight yelled angrily. A spark of magical energy spat out of Twilight's horn, looking almost like Tempest's.

Twilight watched, but the sight of Pinkie Pie and the rest of her friends trotting away was blurry from the tears in her eyes. She had ruined everything by trying to steal the pearl. There was no way to save Equestria now. Twilight fell into a sad, crying heap of a pony. She didn't even notice the dark clouds gathering above her, or realise their implications.

At least Spike had hung back to make sure Twilight was OK. Otherwise no one might have seen the princess get carted away in a cage by Tempest and her guards …

"Twilight!" Spike cried as his friend disappeared into the hull of the skiff. He shot a sad blast of fire at the ship in a feeble attempt to do something to help. But it made no difference. Without her friends, Twilight hadn't stood a chance. The ponies had been officially divided and conquered.

CHAPTER 21

Open Up Your Eyes

Tempest paced around Twilight's cage with a spring in her step. It was the first time Twilight had seen her look anything resembling happy, which was still very sad. "Aw, the Princess of Friendship …" Tempest chuckled. Her hooves clanked noisily on the floor. "… with no friends! And no way out."

"Why are you doing this?" Twilight slumped down. "You're a pony! You're just like me."

Tempest stopped and spun around. She cantered over to Twilight's cage and leaned in close enough for Twilight to see her broken horn. It was jagged and scarred. It looked so painful. "I'm nothing like you," Tempest growled with disdain. "I'm more than you'll ever be."

"Why are you so hateful?" Twilight's eyes searched Tempest's. "I don't understand ..."

Tempest sniffed. Maybe it was time Twilight Sparkle learned a little lesson and got some perspective on what it was like for somepony who hadn't had a perfect life like her. She was just a perfect princess with every chance handed to her on a silver platter with cupcakes next to it.

"I once hoped for friendship, like you." Tempest took a deep breath. "But that was stupid and childish. Because when things got difficult for me, my so-called pony 'friends' abandoned me."

Twilight's eyes grew large. "You had pony friends?"

"Of course I did," Tempest replied. "Fillies don't start out this way." She motioned to her broken horn and sneered. "But they certainly don't want to be around a Unicorn with a broken horn. Even if they were playing in the forest when the ursa minor attacked, too." A tiny spark came from Tempest's horn. "My friends didn't care about me after that. I was too revolting and I couldn't play their little Unicorn games."

"I'm sorry you felt so alone," said Twilight tenderly. She put her hoof up to the bars of her cage to reach out for Tempest, but she shrank back away from the cage.

"I saw the truth. My 'friends' abandoned me when times got tough. And it looks like I'm not the only one." Tempest smiled and began to trot to the door. She turned around and added one last sting before exiting. "Face it, Princess. Friendship has failed you, too."

Alone in her cage, Twilight had realised the actual truth. Friendship hadn't failed her. *Twilight* had failed friendship. She'd grown selfish and put her friends in danger instead of working together to solve the problem, like she'd vowed she'd always do. And there was nothing Twilight could do about it now. The fate of Equestria was in someone else's hooves.

Hours later, Twilight was wheeled into the familiar castle throne room by fellow ponies with chains around their hooves. It was an awful feeling to enter her old home as a prisoner. But it was worse to see the other princesses frozen in stone and the Storm King sitting on the throne.

"Wow, it's a good thing they're stone, right? So you don't have to see their disappointment in your complete, utter failure." Tempest laughed.

Twilight whimpered at the nightmare scene. "Tempest, don't do this! Give the Storm King—"

"Your magic?" Tempest's horn crackled. "Did you think you'd keep it all to yourself? Time to share." The evil pony smiled and looked out the window dreamily. "I'd love for everypony out there to know what I can really do!"

"Ooo, fascinating!" the Storm King bellowed. "Tell me, sparky, what can you do? Light a little candle with that sparkler horn of yours?" He cackled at his nasty comment like it was the funniest thing ever uttered. Tempest shrank back in embarrassment. Twilight actually felt a tiny bit bad for her. The Storm King gestured with his staff at Twilight Sparkle. "Why is this one still moving?"

Tempest gathered herself and remained professional. "She and her friends put up a bit of a fight, but she's alone now. She won't be a problem."

The Storm King lumbered across the room, looking around at the beautiful stained glass windows and tapestries. "Yeah, so, speaking of problems. This place. It seems a little too – oh, I don't know … cute! I don't like cute, I never did like cute – doesn't really go with my whole big bad powerful magic guy thing, does it? Deliver the punchline, Tempest, because this has gotta be a joke!"

The beast slammed his staff to the floor. Instantly, it began to rattle and shake with power as streams of magical energy started to sap from each princess statue. Twilight gritted her teeth, trying to resist the magical pull of the object, but it was so strong. Her horn sputtered and glowed as the magic swirled around the floor and rose up to dance around the Storm King.

The staff glowed brightly. It was fully charged.

"Wow! Let's get this storm started!" the Storm King yelled with glee. "Ooh, hey, that's good, I should trademark that." He shot a jolt of energy at the wall and it came crashing down. Debris flew across the room and into Twilight's cage. She ducked and squinted her eyes, feeling pain at the destruction of her beloved castle.

"Not bad. Actually, kind of first rate! What else does it do?" the Storm King asked Tempest, admiring his new toy.

Tempest followed him and approached him, meekly. "Your Excellency, you promised to restore my horn, and give it even greater power—"

"You gotta be kidding me!" he interrupted, waving the staff around with reckless abandon. "I can move the SUN? AH HAH HAH! WHOA, and the moon!" The Storm King moved both heavenly bodies around in the sky, creating a continual hyper-fast day and night dance.

"Day night, night day, night day night day night sunrise sunset ... de de bup bup bup bah bah bah bah ..." the beast sang. Tempest looked annoyed and impatient. But Twilight realised that all of this dawdling could be useful. Maybe she still had time to come up with a plan.

If only her friends were here.

CHAPTER 22
Battle of Canterlot

Applejack, Rainbow Dash, Pinkie Pie,
Fluttershy and Rarity had been shocked
when Spike came running breathlessly up
to them to deliver the horrible news of
Twilight's kidnapping. But it had been
even more of a shock when Capper,
Captain Celaeno and Princess Skystar
had appeared shortly afterwards at

Mount Aris, hoping to help the ponies. Once they'd told everyone what had happened, they all seemed to grow even more fired up and ready to take back Canterlot. The Storm King just couldn't go on terrorising them – not without a fight! Plus, they had to save Twilight!

Between the cunning skills of Capper; the swashbuckling abilities of the pirates; and Princess Skystar's unwavering positivity and Hippogriff agility, the ragtag team had been able to put together a solid plan for infiltrating the enemy headquarters.

And it was time.

When they arrived at Canterlot, two Storm Creature guards stood in front of Canterlot's main gates. They appeared to be of the standard oaf variety – fond of holding spears and grunting a lot, but that was about it. Capper adjusted his baker disguise, pushed his gigantic 'cake' along and smirked at his own genius. If this little plan didn't work, then he wasn't a cat named Capper. The ponies bound in 'shackles' who were with him really sold the whole story.

As soon as they got close, the guards blocked them with their spears. But Capper was unfazed. He pretended to consult his delivery clipboard.

"All right then. Can one of y'all go and tell your boss he's not getting his 'Congratulations on subduing defenceless pastel ponies' cake?" Capper tapped his toe impatiently. "'Cause I don't want to be the one responsible for the big guy missing his special dessert, you know what I'm sayin'?"

The two guards looked at one another for an answer, shrugged and stepped aside. It was working! Pinkie Pie couldn't help smiling as they trotted into Canterlot. It was easy as pie!

"Pinkie, quit lookin' so happy! Y'ain't foolin' nopony!" Applejack barked under her breath.

Pinkie nodded and put on a dramatic sad face for the rest of the trip to the centre of Canterlot. The plan was to go straight to the castle and attack from the inside, but once they'd arrived at the main square, Grubber happened to see the giant cake. The treat-loving creature ambled over to the cake greedily.

"Hello, cake!" he said, climbing on to the cart to snag a taste of the confection.

"Don't mind if I do." His little paw grabbed a fistful of icing and cake – revealing a set of eyes behind it! "Who puts eyeballs in icing?" Grubber wondered aloud.

Before he could call for the guards, a gaggle of giant birds sprang from the cake! They burst forth and lunged for the Storm Creatures, entangling themselves in a full-on battle! Skystar, now in her Hippogriff form, accompanied Pinkie Pie and the other ponies, flinging cupcake cannonballs and taking out several Storm Creatures of their own. The entire kingdom looked like a big mess of hooves, fur and feathers and soon the Storm Creatures were retreating in fear from the ferocious band of ragtag scallywags!

Capper had done it. They had begun to take back Canterlot.

CHAPTER 23
Storm of the Century

The commotion down below reached up to the tallest towers of the castle. When they heard the sound of the Storm Creatures surrendering, Tempest darted from the throne room to the balcony in disbelief. "What?" she cried, watching the destruction. "How?"

Twilight gasped as she looked down.

"It's … it's the magic of—"

"Yeah, yeah!" the Storm King mocked, making his voice high-pitched and silly. He leaned down and pulled Tempest and Twilight into an insincere embrace. "Friendship and flowers and ponies and … bleeeehhhhh!" He straightened up, a menacing look in his eyes. "I'm so totally over the cute pony thing!" The Storm King raised his staff to the darkening sky. "THIS ENDS NOW!"

A zap of lightning shot straight up from the end of the staff to the heavens. The black clouds moved in, covering the entire sky above Canterlot. A whoosh of wind barrelled through the kingdom, kicking up dust and twisting it into a gigantic tornado. "Yeah!" The Storm King cackled. He was a maniac! And he had nothing to lose.

Twilight wanted to do something, but it was as if her hooves were frozen in place. With the Staff of Sacanas under his control, the Storm King was so powerful. All Twilight could do was to look on in horror as her home was about to be destroyed.

On the ground below, Capper and the crew ran for cover. "Move your hooves, ponies!" he shouted as the tornado began to pick up Storm Creatures and all kinds of other debris.

Rainbow Dash couldn't tear her eyes away from the twister. "You'd have to be faster than a speeding Pegasus to break through that wind!"

Pinkie's eyes widened with intrigue. "Excellent idea, Rainbow Dash!" She whipped out a crash helmet and secured it tightly over her curly fuchsia mane.

If there was ever a time to attempt something like this, it was now. All Pinkie had to do was find some helpers first …

The sound of the Storm King's booming voice echoed right through the chaos. "Now I truly am the Storm King!" He threw his hairy white arms out in triumph. "And the entire world will bow to my va va va **VOOM, BABY!**" His laughter pierced Tempest's ears and she shuddered. She had endured his behaviour long enough. It was her time now.

The plum pony stepped forward to make her case. "Yes, yes, you are every bit as powerful as I promised, sire.

Now, restore my horn and I swear to use my magic to serve you!" She bent her forehoof and bowed down to the beast. But her request was met with maniacal cackles.

"Who cares about your dinky little Unicorn horn?" the Storm King bellowed. He pushed Tempest aside as if she were yesterday's rubbish.

Tempest shook her head in disbelief. Tears began to well up in her eyes. "But we had an agreement …"

"Get with the programme." His broad chest bounced up and down as he laughed. "I used you. It's kinda what I do!" The Storm King raised the staff and pointed it at Tempest. Blasts of magic energy shot towards her and the pony stumbled back, straight into the eye of the tornado! Tempest grabbed on to the balcony railing with her hoof and gripped it for dear life, but it was no use. It was a fitting end for a pathetic, useless Unicorn without a horn or a single friend in the world.

CHAPTER 24

What Friends Do

"Hold on!" Twilight Sparkle shouted over the roar of the worsening storm. Tempest might have been against her this entire time, but there was no way Twilight Sparkle could stand by and watch this happen to her. The princess galloped over and reached her hoof out to her captor.

Tempest's big aqua eyes searched Twilight's. "Why are you saving me?"

"Because this ... is what friends do!" Twilight reached both of her hooves to Tempest and yanked her back on to the balcony. The ponies tumbled to the floor with an unceremonious clash.

By the time the two ponies had picked themselves up, the Storm King was back. He towered over them, pointing the staff directly at their terrified faces. But he was interrupted by a strange sound.

"Wheeeeeeeeeeee!" A shrill shriek of excitement rang out. Pinkie Pie, Applejack, Fluttershy, Rarity, Rainbow Dash and Spike came barrelling through the air right towards the balcony! They landed in an ungraceful heap, knocking the Storm King's staff out of his hands! Everypony groaned in pain except Pinkie.

She immediately sprang to her hooves and shouted triumphantly. "Bullseye!"

"You came back!" Twilight rushed over. She had never been so glad to see her friends. She began to replay the events that had led them there in her mind. "I'm so sorry! I was wrong to—"

Pinkie Pie gave her a sad smile. "I'm sorry, too. Friends mess up sometimes but we never should—"

"Uh, guys, can you make up later?" Rainbow Dash flew over them in a panic. "This isn't over!" She gestured to the Storm King, who had scrambled inside the throne room. The staff was now lodged in the stained glass window. It was wildly out of control, sending even stronger zaps of lightning magic across the space. It shot a blast at the ceiling and chunks of marble and stone began to shatter and fall around them. The ponies darted out of the way of the falling debris, looks of horror and panic upon their faces.

"I've got to get control of it!" Twilight shouted, moving in closer. The strong winds caused her mane to whip around. Time was running out before her beloved Canterlot would crumble to dust.

"You've got this, Twilight," Pinkie shouted over the strengthening storm. Applejack nodded in support.

"No!" Twilight puffed out her chest. "We've got this. Together." That gave her an idea! Of course – the friends had always been stronger as a unit than individually. Now was no different.

Twilight reached for Pinkie Pie's hoof and instantly the ponies were transformed into a powerful chain, swaying in the strong winds. They held on tight to the ground by Applejack's lasso.

It was working!

Now when she reached her hoof out, Twilight could almost reach the staff!

"The staff belongs to ME!" the Storm King bellowed as he hurried over the stones. The window began to crack from the magical pressure. It would shatter at any second. "The power is mine!" The Storm King made one last attempt at seizing the staff by hurling himself at the weakening glass.

But the storm was way too strong. The glass shattered – and both Twilight and the Storm King were sucked into the vortex of scary, violent winds.

"NOOOO!" Pinkie Pie cried out for her friend in anguish. But Twilight Sparkle was gone!

CHAPTER 25
Crashing Down

A blinding flash of light pierced through the clouds and with it, a calm washed over Canterlot. The storm was over. Everything was still, but the ponies couldn't tear their eyes away from the spot where Twilight had disappeared. Fluttershy's eyes were wet with tears as she exchanged a look with a distraught Rarity. Their best friend couldn't be gone for ever … could she? The idea was almost too much to bear.

Then, from high above, Twilight appeared, still clutching the staff! She was the picture of a princess – regal and serene. Everypony cheered as Twilight descended and was immediately enveloped in a group hug. Tempest hung nearby, watching their friendship with wonder. Before Twilight had saved her, Tempest couldn't imagine feeling the way they all did about each other. Now, she understood.

Tempest was the first to see the Storm King pulling himself up on to the balcony. "I'm not done yet!" he mumbled under his breath. The ponies were so distracted that they didn't notice him pulling out a spare Obsidian Orb and gearing up to throw it at Twilight.

"Nooooo!" Tempest shouted as she leapt over the ponies and straight into the line of fire. Once the orb made contact, it exploded in a dramatic cloud of magical smoke. Tempest and the Storm King both froze in mid-air as their bodies became completely made of stone.

Unable to move, the Storm King fell back over the edge of the balcony and went crashing to the ground below. The stone broke apart into a thousand tiny pieces. But Tempest was frozen and caught in a magic bubble, surrounding by the glittering purple magic of Twilight's horn. The princess lowered her gently on to the balcony. Rainbow Dash shook her head in sheer amazement.

"Whoa, I can't believe she did that!"

"I can," Twilight admitted, unable to hide her proud smile. The princess grabbed on to the staff and encouraged her friends to do the same. All six ponies and Spike shared the weight of it, pointing the powerful beam directly at Tempest.

Slowly, the Unicorn's body returned to its normal colour. Tempest was able to move once more. The look of surprise on her face said everything. Tempest was new to this whole friendship thing, but Princess Twilight Sparkle had a feeling she was going to like it.

"Now what?" Fluttershy wondered aloud.

"Now, we fix everything," Twilight said, feeling hopeful. Her home was not ruined. The magic from the staff was powerful enough to undo all the destruction the Storm King had caused. And that's exactly what Twilight did.

Chapter 26
The Friendship Serenade

Canterlot was looking gorgeous, thanks
to the helping hooves of everypony in the
Kingdom. There wasn't a single cloud in
the sky and the sun shone down on the
Friendship Festival stage, lighting it with a
golden glow that even magic couldn't
create. The throngs of ponies stomped
their hooves in excitement as a small

dragon took to the stage.

"Fillies and Gentlecolts!" Spike shouted to the huge crowd. "Get ready for … Songbird Serenade!"

The pop star gave a big smile and waved. "And now, to celebrate the fact that we're all still here in one piece – give it up for Princess Twilight and her friends!" Songbird  motioned to where Twilight, Rarity, Applejack, Fluttershy, Rainbow Dash, Pinkie Pie and Spike stood together off to the side of the stage. The ponies blushed at the sound of deafening applause and cheering.

As the party raged on throughout the afternoon and well into the evening, the spirit of the festival could be seen everywhere. Friends new and old were busy having fun together. Capper and Rarity chatted about her surprise gift to him (a new coat); Pinkie Pie and Princess Skystar shared cupcakes and giggles; and Rainbow Dash and her new pal Captain Celaeno exchanged stories of awesomeness and adventures. Spike was getting along surprisingly well with Grubber, and Queen Novo even joined the celebration with some of her Hippogriff friends!

There was only one pony who didn't seem to be enjoying herself. Twilight trotted over to Tempest and gave her a smile.

"That's one thing that never changes around here ... ponies like a party." Tempest said with a smile.

"Well, I hope you'll stay," Twilight said warmly. "More friends are definitely merrier!"

Tempest slumped down with a heavy sigh. "But what about my broken horn?" Her voice broke the tiniest bit when she said it. Even with all the merriment around her, Tempest was still hung up on something that made her special.

"You know," Twilight admitted, "your horn is pretty powerful, just like the pony it belongs to."

At this, a hint of a genuine smile began to form on Tempest's face. Nopony had ever complimented her broken horn before. It could do some unique things. Maybe it was time to share them.

"I've been wanting to show everypony in Equestria what I can do …" Tempest conceded. She summoned her magical strength and shot off some crackling sparks from her horn. They zoomed up high into the sky and exploded into the most brilliant, fizzling fireworks!

"Nice touch, Tempest!" Pinkie Pie called out as she bounced over. Fluttershy trotted behind her.

"Actually, Tempest isn't my real name …" Tempest said with a small, sheepish shrug.

"Ooooh!" Pinkie Pie squealed. "What is it?"

Applejack, Rarity and Rainbow Dash trotted over and crowded in, hoping to hear as well. Tempest really was a pony of mystery! She motioned for them all to get closer before whispering. "Uh, my real name is … Fizzlepop Berrytwist." Tempest's eyes were wide with embarrassment.

"OK!" Pinkie Pie gasped. "That is the most awesome name EVER!"

Everypony erupted into giggles and nodded in agreement. For the first time in ages, Tempest joined in, too. She might have forgotten what the magic of friendship felt like, but she never would do again.

The End

Do you want to know more about Tempest Shadow?

Find out about her life before she met the Storm King in *Tempest's Story*, the prequel to *My Little Pony: The Movie*.

Turn over for a sneak peek!

Tempest's Story

A young Unicorn walked through the
forest, her two best friends right beside her.
Glitter Drops and Spring Rain were
Unicorns, too, and together, the three of
them liked to practise their magic. Every
morning they'd venture out into the forest,
or explore the mountains by their town,
taking a break now and then to play ball.

"There it is," the young Unicorn said as they stepped into the clearing. She stared into the sky. Canterlot was high above them. The capital of Equestria was perched in the mountains and could be seen for miles around. The three friends had never actually been there, but they'd heard hundreds of stories about it. The city was filled with ivory towers and waterfalls, shimmering spires and majestic views. But most importantly, it was the home of two of the three princesses, and a common spot for them to meet.

The three princesses were Alicorns – Unicorns with powerful wings. Princess Celestia and Princess Luna controlled the sun and the moon, and Princess Cadance was the ruler of the Crystal Empire. She had once been Princess Celestia's apprentice.

"Do you think we'll ever get to Canterlot?" Spring Rain asked.

"Of course we will," the young Unicorn said.

"And who knows ..." Glitter Drops smiled. "Maybe one of us will become a princess one day, too!"

"But first, Princess Celestia's School for Gifted Unicorns," the young Unicorn said, "where all the most talented Unicorns learn to focus their powerful magic. We'll get there some day; I know we will."

The young Unicorn couldn't admit it to even her closest friends, but she thought about Princess Celestia's school every single day. She dreamed about studying in Canterlot, learning to make magic that glowed and sparked with power. She'd work as hard as she could to make Princess Celestia proud. Sometimes she even imagined becoming an Alicorn herself.

Would she ever be given wings? Could she ever be that powerful?

There were entrance exams every spring. The young Unicorn hoped she'd be ready when they came around one moon. She wanted to attend the school, as soon as she could. It was hard waiting for something you wanted so much.

"Let's practise," she said, turning to Glitter Drops and Spring Rain. "Let's levitate the ball."

Glitter Drops's horn sparked and glowed. She took the ball from her satchel and sent it flying off into the woods. The young Unicorn darted after it, weaving in and out of the trees. She could just see the ball up ahead, glowing in the air. It was like the bouncy balls other ponies tossed back and forth, only this one was special.

If she focused her magic, she could make it float and glow with a beautiful white light. It looked like the moon.

"I can't keep up!" Glitter Drops called out. She was running as fast as she could through the forest, but the ball was always a little ahead of her. She laughed as she ran, clearly enjoying the way the wind felt in her mane.

Spring Rain darted out in front of the young Unicorn. She raced across the ground to the ball, but she stumbled and fell. She hadn't been concentrating hard enough, but that wasn't her fault. It was tough to concentrate on magic, run really fast and keep your eyes on the ball.

The young Unicorn galloped out in front of both of her friends. The ball was up ahead.

She was so close. She just had to run

a little bit faster …

"Where'd it go?" Spring Rain's voice called out. "It disappeared!"

The young Unicorn stopped at the mouth of a cave. The ball had floated inside. She could still see the glowing light, but it was dimmer now. The ball was somewhere in there, deep in the mountain.

"Oh no …," Glitter Drops stopped right behind her. She peered inside. The cave was so dark they couldn't see past the opening. "Who's going to go and get it?"

Glitter Drops and Spring Rain turned to their brave friend. The purple Unicorn was the youngest, but she was always the bravest of the three. She'd talked to the hydra when they went to Froggy Bottom Bogg, and she had found her way through the Everfree Forest on her own. Whenever something scary happened, her friends always looked to her first.

"I'll be right back," the young Unicorn said. Then she ventured into the cave, trying to follow the dim light from the ball.

Inside, she could hardly see anything. The ball was somewhere up ahead, around a sharp corner, but she couldn't make out the floor of the cave. She stumbled over a rock and fell, landing hard. When she finally got up, her shoulder hurt.

"This isn't as easy as I thought it would be …" she said to herself, rubbing the sore spot on her side. She went slower now, being careful with each step. "Just a little further …"

She was getting closer. As she turned the corner, she saw the ball floating in the air. That whole part of the cave was lit up now. She could see everything perfectly.

It looked like some creature had been

living there. There were scraps of food and a warm, cosy bed. She reached up, grabbed the ball and tucked it behind her front leg. But when she turned back around, there was an ursa minor standing right in front of her.

She didn't have time to react. The huge bear roared in her face. She ducked underneath its foreleg, trying to get away, but it chased after her. She didn't move more than a few feet before it struck her with its giant paw. She went flying across the cave, her head knocking into the wall.

She got up as fast as she could, knowing the bear would be right behind her. As she got closer to the entrance of the cave, she could see Glitter Drops and Spring Rain waiting for her. They were both staring inside the cave, trying to see what was happening.

"Run!" she yelled. "There's an ursa minor!"

Spring Rain and Glitter Drops turned around and darted off through the forest. The young Unicorn followed them, relieved when she was finally out of the cave. She'd dropped the ball at some point along the way, but it didn't matter. She had to get as far away from the ursa minor as she could.

She didn't stop running until she was out of the forest and saw Spring Rain and Glitter Drops standing in the field up ahead. She turned back, looking into the trees to make sure they were safe. After all that, they were finally alone. The bear hadn't followed them.

"I went all the way to the back of the cave," the young Unicorn said. "I found the ball, but then, when I turned around, the ursa minor was right behind me. It chased me, and then I fell, and then ..."

Glitter Drops and Spring Rain just stared at her. Their eyes were wide, and their expressions were serious. They looked like something was horribly wrong. The young Unicorn glanced down at her hooves, making sure she wasn't hurt. She looked over her shoulder at her tail and mane. Everything seemed fine.

"I don't think I'm hurt," she said. "Just a few scratches ..."

"I don't know how to tell you this ..." Glitter Drops said, her eyes watering. "It's your horn."

The young Unicorn reached up and touched the front of her head. Her horn was just a small, jagged stump. The top half had broken off.

Her eyes immediately filled with tears.

"No," she said, shaking her head. "No! It can't be. What's a Unicorn without her horn?"

"I'm so sorry." Glitter Drops hugged her friend.

"It'll be OK," Spring Rain added, wrapping her front leg around the young Unicorn's other side.

The tears streamed down the young Unicorn's cheeks. She'd lost her horn. All her magic was contained within it. How would anything ever be OK again?

The young Unicorn and her two friends set off through town, Spring Rain walking on one side of her and Glitter Drops walking on the other. She'd waited weeks, then months, for her horn to grow back, but nothing had happened. This was the first time the Unicorn had left her house since the day at the cave, but Spring Rain and Glitter Drops had told her it would be OK. She still couldn't help but feel nervous, though. Every time she looked at her broken horn she started crying.

Read

Tempest's Story

to find out what happens next!

Explore the magical world of My Little Pony!

Collect all the My Little Pony Early Readers

Are you the ultimate My Little Pony fan?

Packed with all the fun, facts and magic of My Little Pony, this is a must-have guide to the world of Equestria.

Don't miss out on the Ultimate Guide!

Contents

Underworld

The first story:

Overworld

Chapter One:
Away for the summer

You had to have keen eyes to spot the well. Older eyes would strain to get a glimpse, but they always failed. All they saw was darkness and shadow. The sharpest eyes might think they glimpsed a movement here, a trick of the light there, but never more than that. Even young men and young women searched in vain for it. Truth is, only a child was likely to find it, and a very special child at that, one who didn't just look, but saw.

A slimy, moss-covered board covered the well. The board was rotten, but it had looked that way for many years, maybe even centuries. Year after year it looked as rotten as it always had, but it never quite rotted away. Had it always been like that? Nobody had been around long enough to know.

To get to the well you set off along Owl Heart Lane and turned left. A winding path brought you to a rickety wooden bridge. You then followed a rough track around the edge of Farmer Sutch's field. Trample his crops and he would come after you with his shotgun, or so the villagers said, though he had never shot anyone as far as they knew, only the odd pigeon or crow. From there you went along the river and through a water meadow. On the far side of the meadow you would find the thicket and at the heart of that was the well. It was quite a trek for a grown up and a great journey for a child, but for those who completed the quest there was a great prize, a reward beyond his or her wildest dreams.

Will Antrobus didn't know any of this the summer he went to stay with his grandparents. He was just an ordinary nine-year-old boy, or so he thought. There had been nothing in his life so far to say otherwise. He did the usual things boys do. He got up, ate his breakfast and sometimes two of them. He went to school and played football on the yard. He came home and played football with his Dad. He was a moderately good boy so he usually did what the teachers said. He understood most of the stuff they taught him and didn't let on about the stuff he didn't.

"Why have I got to stay with Gran and Granddad this summer?" he grumbled as the village flashed past, the old Norman church, the Bear's Paw pub, the shop that was also a post office and the old, stone cross in the square. "Two whole weeks! Jack and I had all kinds of things planned."

Jack was his best friend. They didn't have anything planned, but Mum wasn't to know that.

"Your dad and I need to sort some things out," she told him.

"What things?"

"Just things," she said. "Don't ask so many questions."

Will knew there was no point asking questions or pleading to go home. They were nearly there. It was a done deal. So he didn't protest or grumble. He didn't complain at all. Instead, he just stared out of the window and sulked quietly. It was easy to miss Gran and Granddad's cottage. It was set back off the road. A giant oak tree concealed the entrance to the drive. Its branches hung over the gate. Of course, Mum knew exactly where to turn. She had grown up in the little, thatched cottage two minutes from the centre of the village. Twigs tapped and squealed on the roof as she hung a left off the main road. For a moment all Will could see was the sunlight peeking through the deep green tangle of leaves then there it was, his grandparents' cottage.

Gran and Granddad had heard the car tyres crunching on the pebbled drive and they came out to greet their daughter and grandson. They were standing in the doorway where ivy climbed. They didn't look old, not the way grandparents look in storybooks. They didn't even have grey hair, at least not so much you'd notice. Gran had a shock of coppery hair with just a few threads of grey. Granddad's hair was black on top and grey at the sides, which made him look a bit like a badger. So if you are looking for grey, stooped grandparents with shaky voices, you are going to be disappointed.

"Hello, Will," Gran said. "How's my favourite grandson?"

"You don't have any other grandchildren," Will said pointedly.

Gran laughed. Granddad frowned. He seemed to think that was a bit of a cheeky thing to say. Granddad didn't say very much. Gran did enough talking for the both of them. He just tousled Will's hair, which was coppery like Mum's and Gran's, and lifted the boy's suitcase out of the boot.

"I'll put the kettle on," Gran said. "What will you have, Will? We've got orange juice or cranberry juice."

Will asked for a can of cola, but Gran shook her head.

"Fizzy drinks aren't good for children," she said. "They make you- oh, I don't know-"

"Fizzy?" Will asked.

"Yes, fizzy, that's it. I don't like fizzy children. They are too bubbly by half as it is. The bubbles go to straight to their heads. Then they get up to all kinds of mischief."

Will didn't think fizzy drinks made him do anything out of the ordinary, but he didn't say so.

"Orange then, please," he said, thinking that nobody could get up to mischief in a sleepy village like Greengate, but he always remembered his manners, even when he was in a sulk. "Can I watch some TV?"

Granddad frowned again. He didn't think TV was good for growing boys. He thought they should be out climbing trees or damming streams the way he did when he was a boy. That's what he always said. Boys ought to be out of the house and roaming the countryside. This particular day, he didn't say any such thing. He handed Will the remote control. But he still frowned.

While Will watched TV Mum and Gran vanished into the parlour. He could hear them talking above the noise of the TV, but he couldn't make out the words. He guessed that it was about Mum and Dad and the things they had to sort out. Granddad sat in his armchair reading a book so Will couldn't turn down the volume to eavesdrop. After about twenty minutes Mum emerged from the parlour.

"I'll have to go now," she said. "Give me a big Will hug."

Will gave her a huge hug and watched her go. He saw the brake lights flash when she reached the main road. It made him kind of sad to be left alone in the middle of nowhere, which is the way he thought of Greengate. As he went back indoors he was still wondering what these things were that she had to sort out with Dad.

Chapter Two
The Well

The owl took Will by surprise. He got up about eight o'clock, had sausage, eggs, bacon, tomatoes and mushrooms for breakfast then went back to his room, and there it was, a large brown owl watching him through the window. It made Will jump. When he had got over his surprise he stared back at the owl. The owl wasn't surprised at all and it certainly wasn't in any mood to jump. It simply stared back at Will. It was as if it was examining him very carefully. It seemed to want something from him but, as it couldn't talk, whatever it wanted remained a mystery.

"Shoo," Will said. "Go."

The owl didn't go.

"Shoo!"

Still the owl didn't move. Will threw his dirty socks at the window. The owl continued to watch him for a few moments, more carefully than ever, or at least that's how it appeared. Then it spread its wings and flew away. Will raced to the window and watched it go. It swooped down Owl Heart Lane and turned left.

"That's odd," Will said out loud, "an owl flying down Owl Heart Lane. Whatever next, a pig flying down Pig Heart Lane?"

He raced downstairs to tell his grandparents.

"There was an owl," he said. "It was right outside my window, staring at me."

Neither of them seemed a bit surprised.

"That sort of thing happens round here," Granddad said.

"But it's broad daylight," Will said. "The sun is out."

"People can be contrary," Gran said. "Maybe some owls are too."

Will couldn't understand why they weren't more surprised by the owl's behaviour. He remembered the way the owl flew down Owl Heart Lane and turned left.

"What's down there?" he asked, pointing out of the window.

He explained that the owl had flown down Owl Heart Lane and turned left.

"It takes you to a bridge," Gran said. "It leads you to Farmer Sutch's cornfield. If you're thinking of going to explore, don't trample his crops. He's got a shotgun."

"Does he shoot boys?" Will asked.

"He hasn't shot any yet," Gran said. "But you never know."

Will thought she was teasing, but he wasn't quite sure.

"Do you mind if I go and have a look around?" he asked.

"You run along," said Gran. "I will make you a packed lunch to take with you. Just make sure you're back by sunset. We don't want you losing your way."

Will was surprised that she didn't warn him about traffic and strangers. When he was home with Mum and Dad he got a lecture every time he went down to the shops. They made the neighbourhood sound like a dangerous place. He was starting to realise that his grandparents were very different. Gran handed him a small rucksack that he slipped over his shoulders. He was almost out of the door when Granddad called to him. Here it comes, thought Will. Watch out for traffic. Don't talk to strangers. But Granddad didn't say anything of the kind.

"When you go exploring," he said, "it's important to keep your eyes peeled. Just because you don't see something right away, it doesn't mean it isn't there. You remember that."

"I will, Granddad," Will said. "Thank you."

He wasn't quite sure what he was thanking Granddad for, but he thought he ought to. He walked briskly down Owl Heart Lane. It felt like the beginning of a great adventure. The sun bobbed along behind the oak and yew trees. Far, far away, traffic rumbled. At the end of Owl Heart Lane, he turned left just the way the owl had. A winding path led to the rickety bridge Gran had mentioned. He glanced briefly at the sluggish stream where dragonflies darted before entering Farmer Sutch's cornfield. He took care to stick to the rough track around the edge. He didn't want to be shot like a pigeon or a crow. When he reached the far side he frowned. He had the strangest feeling he knew this place, but he had never been here before. He thought about it for a little while, but he couldn't come up with an explanation for it so he continued his walk.

He wandered along the riverbank, stopping from time to time to peer through the thick bushes at the flowing water. There were coots and moorhens and ducks. Bullrushes waved in the breeze. Flies hummed on the surface. He realised it was the first time he had ever gone further than Owl Heart Lane. Usually he played in his grandparents' garden or walked down to the village with them to buy groceries. Now here he was, all on his own, a long, long way from their thatched cottage.

He started to cross the water meadow. There were nodding purple flowers and swaying grasses with feathery heads. He found it very mysterious and new. There was no path or track so walking was difficult. He had to lift his feet and bend his knees. It made his legs ache. That's when he saw the thicket. There were lots of trees and bushes, but there was something about the shape of this one. It reminded him of the lych-gate of Greengate Church. It seemed to invite you in.

He ran across excitedly, expecting to find something special. He peered inside, but there was nothing but shadow and gloom. He felt so disappointed. Then he remembered what Granddad had said: just because you don't see something right away, it doesn't mean it isn't there. So he leaned inside. He looked left. He looked right. He edged forward, pulling back the branches that snapped back and slapped him. Still he couldn't see anything interesting. No, wait. What was that? He ducked under a hanging branch and twisted to his left. There, quite hidden, he discovered a kind of winding passage formed by the tangled branches. At the end of the passage the sunlight showed through.

It took a moment or two before he could see properly. After spending a few minutes in the dark of the thicket, the sudden flash of sunlight almost blinded him. When his vision cleared he found himself looking at a stone well. A rotting, slimy board covered it. But there was something else, something that made him think he was seeing things. Perched on the board was a garden gnome, the kind people had in their gardens, and it seemed to be looking right at him.

Chapter Three
Nimbus

Will stared at the gnome for a while and decided he was imagining it. How could a gnome stare at anything or anyone? Its eyes weren't real. They were just blue paint on white pottery. It wasn't a living thing at all. It was just a little statue made of fired clay. But what was it doing out here in a deserted spot in the middle of the countryside? People usually had gnomes in their garden. They didn't leave them sitting on a well in a thicket on the far side of an overgrown meadow. This was hidden so well you had to be really determined to find it. It didn't make any sense.

15

The gnome was thirty centimetres tall, about the height of a school ruler. It was dressed in a jaunty, scarlet cap, a scarlet waistcoat over a white shirt and black trousers and boots. It had a long, white beard like Father Christmas and sparkling, aquamarine eyes. It held a fishing rod in its podgy, pink hands.

"Fancy meeting you here," Will said.

Then, wondering what he was doing talking to a garden gnome, he started to slide the board back so he could look into the well. The board was surprisingly heavy, but he managed to shove it halfway. There wasn't much to see. Even with the help of the dappled sunlight through the branches, he could only just make out the dark water far below. Disappointed not to have found something more interesting, he slid the board back. He decided to take one more look at the gnome.

"You look so real," he said then turned to go.

"So do you," came a voice.

Will spun round.

"Who said that?" he croaked, really rather scared.

He tugged at the bushes. Somebody must be watching him from a hiding place. No matter how he searched, he didn't find anyone. He frowned then stared at the gnome for the longest time before deciding he must have been hearing things. Once more he set off in the direction of his grandparents' cottage. This time he got about five steps then he heard the voice again.

"You give up easily."

"OK," Will said, "who *is* that?"

He was getting annoyed.

"Come on, I mean it. Show yourself."

"It's not difficult to find me if you really want to," the voice said.

Will retraced his steps. He noticed something really strange. The gnome had been sitting cross-legged on the well the first time he saw it. Now it had its legs apart, with its heels pressed against the brickwork. It had moved. Either that, or somebody had swapped this gnome for another one. But how could anyone have done it? There was only one way into the thicket and one way out. Besides, nobody had made the slightest sound. It would have been impossible to sneak in and swap the gnomes without making a noise. The branches and briars were so entangled even a rabbit or a fox would have found it hard to push its way through.

"You moved!" Will said.

"So?" the gnome said. "You did too."

"But I'm a boy," Will said. "I'm supposed to move."

"And I'm a gnome," the gnome said. "Why shouldn't I move too?"

Will had no answer than that. He didn't say anything for a moment so the gnome did the talking. Will watched in amazement as its mouth opened and closed.

"You can talk!"

"Obviously."

"This is so cool."

"Actually, the day is rather warm," the gnome said, glancing up at the sky.

"No, you don't understand," Will explained. "Cool means good."

"So why didn't you say good?" the gnome asked.

"It's the way we talk where I come from."

"It's a silly way to talk," the gnome grunted. "You must come from somewhere silly."

"I come from London."

"Then London must be silly. You should say what you mean and mean what you say. I call a gnome a gnome and a boy a boy. Why do you say something good is *cool*?"

Will decided they were getting off the point.

"But you *talked*!"

"You keep saying that. What's so special about talking?"

"Nothing," Will said, "so long as you're a human. But gnomes don't talk. They're not...alive."

The gnome scrambled to its, no his, feet. He started to jump up and down on the board.

"If I'm not alive, how do you explain this?"

Will shrugged his shoulders.

"I can't."

"So you believe I'm alive?"

"Yes."

"You think I'm real?"

"Yes."

"I'm not a figment of your imagination. I'm not a daydream or a trick of the light?"

"No," Will said. "You're quite, quite real."

"Then you are a very special boy," the gnome said.

"Am I? Am I really?"

"You most definitely are. Some children find the thicket, but they can't see the well. Others get as far as the well, but they don't see me. Only the most special children can see the thicket, the well and me."

"Why?"

"Nobody knows, but it's true. You don't come across many three-seers in this world."

"What kind of answer is that?" Will asked.

"It's probably the best answer anyone will ever have for the ways of the world," the gnome said. "There's no explaining them. Some things just are." The gnome reached under his beard and scratched his chin. "This is very interesting, very interesting indeed. What's your name, boy?"

"Will."

The dwarf seemed pleased.

"Will's a good name," he said.

"Thank you," Will said. "So what's yours?"

"Mine?" the dwarf said, as if surprised that he had been asked. "I'm Nimbus."

Chapter Four
The Wish

"Nimbus?"

"That's right."

"Like the clouds?"

Nimbus nodded.

"Yes, like the clouds."

"Why?"

Nimbus gave Will a long, lowering, growly kind of look.

"Why not?"

"You don't name people after clouds."

"Gnome parents do. They name their children after trees, clouds, streams, rivers, flowers….."

"That's silly."

"No, it isn't. Humans do it. There are girls called Rose and Poppy and Willow and Holly."

"What about boys? Got you there, haven't I?"

"Peter means stone," Nimbus said. "There are also boys called things like River."

Will realised he had lost the argument, but he was as stubborn as stone.

"But there are no boys named after clouds."

"Well, there should be."

They glared at each other for a moment or two then burst out laughing.

"I think I'm going to like you, Will. What's your second name?"

"It's Antrobus," Will said. "I am William Thomas Antrobus."

Nimbus' eyes lit up and that was quite something, because they were pretty sparkly to begin with.

"You've got a *bus* at the end of your name. That's good. That's very good. I knew a child with a bus in her name once. She was a brave, little soul."

"Why's it good to have a bus in my name?"

"Nimbus has a bus at the end too."

Will laughed.

"So it does. Is that important?"

"It is very important. People think these things are coincidences, but they're not." He tapped his fleshy nose, which was red and rather lumpy. "They're *patterns*."

He made it sound ever so mysterious.

"How do you mean?"

"Oh, there are all kinds of patterns in the world. There are things that make people say: 'Well, I never!' and 'How odd.'"

"And they're patterns?"

"Some of them are. Some of them aren't. It takes a three-seer like you to spot the real ones."

That made Will feel very important though he didn't really understand all this stuff about three-seers and patterns. But Nimbus was a talking gnome so he was willing to cut the little guy some slack.

"So you're saying there is some kind of link between us because of our names," Will said.

"Could be," Nimbus said. "Could very well be."

Will thought this was probably nonsense, but he didn't say so. He quite wanted there to be some pattern, something special between them.

"Why did your parents call you Nimbus?" he asked.

21

"Because of my beard, of course."

Will started laughing.

"What are you giggling about now, boy?"

"They must have given you your name when you were a baby. Babies don't have beards!"

"Gnome babies do."

"Really? You have beards from the moment you're born?"

"Yes, from the moment our mothers fish us out of the pond, we've got our beards. They are as white and downy as a swan's breast."

Will didn't know what to make of that.

"I think you need to explain what you mean."

"That's how gnome babies are made. There's a gnome mum and a gnome dad. They go to the ceilidh...."

"The what?"

"Haven't your parents told you anything about the old ways?"

"No, not much."

"Well," Nimbus said, taking a very deep breath, the kind of breath you take when you're explaining something really difficult, "the gnome mum takes a shine to the gnome dad so they dance together. The ceilidh is a dance."

"Oh."

"Then some time later, splash, the little gnome baby is swimming round the birthing pond. That's how all gnome babies come into the world."

"It sounds kind of funny," Will said.

"It's kind of dangerous," Nimbus said. "If your mother is a bit slow, some waiting pike might just gobble you up."

"How horrible!"

"Horrible is right. Mr Pike has razor sharp teeth. He'll make short work of a baby gnome."

"So mother gnomes don't go into hospital to have their babies?"

"Hospital?" Nimbus said. "Why would they go there? They're not sick. They're having a baby."

"My mum had me in a hospital."

"Was she sick?"

"No."

"You humans are very odd," Nimbus said. "Why go to hospital if you're not sick?"

Will realised he didn't know the answer to that.

"I don't know."

"Ah well," Nimbus said, "there's no understanding the ways of humans. They're a peculiar breed and no mistake. Let's get down to business, Will Antrobus, what's your wish?"

Will was excited.

"I get a wish!"

"You certainly do. A three-seer gets to make a wish. What's it to be?"

"Do you mind if I think about it?" Will said.

"Take all the time you like," Nimbus said. "You're on holiday for five whole weeks. There's no school to go to. You've got all morning and all afternoon to think about it. You've got to choose your wish before the sun goes down, mind. The moment the light dies, the wish dies with it. You don't want to start making after-dark wishes."

"Why not?"

"Oh, they are always trouble."

So Will sat down on the dry grass and started to think about the wish.

Chapter Five
Wings

Will finally made his mind up.

"Could I have wings?" he asked.

"Chicken wings?" Nimbus asked. "Nice, savoury chicken wings?"

He smacked his lips at the thought.

"No, not chicken wings," Will said, "wings that grow out of my back, wings that will make me fly."

"Now that, Will Antrobus, is a very good choice for a beginner." Nimbus picked up his fishing rod and did the strangest thing. He started to unscrew it. Will didn't understand what he was doing at first then he realised what he was looking at.

"The handle," he said. "It's a wand."

"You've got to have a wand to do magic," Nimbus said. "This one is made of mistletoe."

"Is that good?"

"It's the best."

Nimbus flicked his wrist and drew a pattern in the air. There was a shower of tiny gold sparks and they started to cascade over Will. Immediately he felt a tingle between his shoulder blades.

"Something's happening," Will said excitedly. "Is it my wings?"

"It most certainly is," Nimbus said.

"Cool."

Nimbus frowned.

25

"I mean good," Will said hastily.

The tingling turned to itching then he heard a kind of creaking.

"Is that the sound of them growing?" he asked.

"It is. Let's go down to the river. You will be able to see your reflection in the water."

When they reached the riverbank Will gazed at the surface of the water.

"They're brown!"

"What colour did you expect?"

"Well, white I suppose."

"Angels have white wings. Boys have brown ones."

"Oh. What about girls' wings?"

"They're amber like autumn leaves."

"I thought they would be pink."

"A lot of girls want pink wings, but they always come out amber. You don't always get what you want."

Will looked at his reflection. What was he complaining about? After all, he did have wings even if they were a tawny brown. He started flapping them.

"Whoa, not so fast," Nimbus cried. "You don't want to go soaring into the sky and straight into the engines of a passing aeroplane, do you?"

"No, of course not."

"I once saw a boy sliced like bacon in the propellor of a Sopwith Camel."

"How awful! What's a Sopwith Camel?"

"An aeroplane from the old days."

Will tried to imagine a Sopwith Camel.

"Just imagine if you got yourself caught in a helicopter's rotor blades."

"That would be bad, wouldn't it?" Will said.

"It would be fatal," Nimbus said. "You would be chopped into slices like a sausage."

All this talk of bacon and sausages was making Will hungry.

"Now, Will Antrobus, listen carefully and I will give you a few pointers. There's more to flying than just flapping your wings, you know."

Will didn't know at all, but he pretended he did.

"Oh, I know."

"Right," Nimbus said, spitting on his palms and rubbing them together, "down to work. Flap slowly, very, very slowly like this."

He demonstrated with his arms. Will copied, but with his wings.

"Look!" he said excitedly. "My feet are off the ground."

They were too. It was only a few centimetres, but he was hovering above the earth.

"Now tilt right like this. See, you can control where you're going. Now left like this. Not so fast. It is all about slow, deliberate movements. Good. Let's try going up."

Will flapped hard, shot into the air and cracked his head on an overhanging branch.

"Ow!"

"Which part of slow and deliberate do you not understand?" Nimbus grumbled. "Now, *slow* and *easy* does it."

After a quarter of an hour's instruction, Will was starting to get the hang of flying.

"Let's try something more ambitious," Nimbus said. "Try going round this tree, across the river, round the willow on the far bank and back again."

Will did as he was told.

"How was that?"

"Perfect," Nimbus said. "You're a natural. OK, off you go. Try flying to the village and back again."

"Won't people see me?"

"What, that lot of one-seers and two-seers? You don't need to worry about them. They don't have a bit of imagination. One-seers only see what's on the surface. Two seers know there is something under the surface, but they don't know what it is. They will tell themselves it was just a bird. Just don't hang around too long. Even a one-seer will spot you if you stand in front of him long enough."

Will couldn't wait to try out his wings. He rose steadily into the air and glanced down at Nimbus.

"That's it, boy. That's it," the gnome shouted encouragingly.

Will soared into the sky. He felt the wind on his face and the air currents lifting his wings. He banked left then right, trying out his new skill. Presently he spotted Greengate church and looped around the steeple.

"So good," he cried. " So *cool!*"

He sped across the village then turned effortlessly before sweeping across Farmer Sutch's cornfield back to Nimbus.

"Very good," Nimbus said. "That was very good indeed. You might need those flying skills before long."

"What do you mean?" Will asked.

"One thing at a time," Nimbus said. "You'll find out soon enough."

Chapter Six
Home before dark

On his return from flying round the village Will sat on the grass and ate his sandwiches. There had been so much excitement he had forgotten that he was meant to get hungry half way through the day. By the time he finished his lunch the sun was sinking over the treetops and the sky had a fiery hue.

"What time is it?" he asked Nimbus.

The gnome examined the scarlet sun as it dipped beneath the treeline.

"It will be dark in just over an hour," he said.

"Don't you go by the time?" Will asked, noticing that Nimbus wasn't wearing a watch.

"I've got no use for seconds and minutes and hours," Nimbus said. "I go by the sun and the moon and the sparkling stars. That's the way it has always been for we woodland folk."

"What about days of the week?"

"No time for them."

"The months then? The years?"

"Sunrise, sunset, spring, summer, autumn, winter, that's all we care about. That's the rhythm of nature, young Will. You don't need any more than that."

That's when Will thought of something that hadn't occurred to him before.

"You keep saying *we*," he said.

"What's your point?"

"Well, I haven't seen anyone else like you."

"Did you ask to see anyone else?"

"Well, no."

"That's why, then."

"So if I asked to meet some of your gnome friends, I could?"

"Maybe," Nimbus said. "It depends."

"Depends on what?"

"Whether they want to meet you. You didn't think of that, did you?"

Will shook his head.

"No, I didn't."

"Well, you should. That's the trouble with humans. Selfish, they are. They think the world revolves around them. Look at the way they treat the land. They go shoving their roads hither and thither like barbed wire, without a thought for the folk living in the woods they tear down and the fields they churn up."

"I've never thought about it like that," Will said.

"Well, you should and so should your parents. Yes, and so should those people in their offices in big cities taking decisions that mess up our woods and meadows. There will come a day when there's nowhere for the woodland folk to live, none at all."

The sun was turning crimson and the trees, hedges and bushes looked almost black against its dying rays.

"I'd better be going," Will said.

"Yes, you'd better get home before you lose the light," Nimbus agreed.

That's when Will's heart thumped in panic.

"What about these?"

He jerked his thumb at the pair of brown wings.

"Don't you worry about them," Nimbus told him. "They'll have faded away by the time you reach the rickety bridge."

"Just like that?"

"Just like that. A day wish only lasts as long as the light of day. The moment the light dies, the wish dies with it."

"You said there were night wishes."

"No, I didn't."

"Yes, you did!"

The question had a strange effect on Nimbus. He gave a little shudder of fright.

"Well, I shouldn't have. Night wishes are dangerous things. You don't go giving them out unless you really have to. Things can go wrong with night wishes."

Will wasn't sure what to make of that.

"I had better be on my way," he said, reassured by the thought that the wings would vanish by themselves. Gran and Granddad wouldn't be very happy if he turned up looking like that owl that came up to his bedroom window.

"Yes, you get yourself home. Your tea will be on the hob."

"Can I come back tomorrow?" Will said.

"You better had," Nimbus said. "You've got a lot to learn."

Will beamed.

"I can't wait," he said. "I'll be here at nine o'clock sharp."

"You'll be here at ten o'clock at the earliest," Nimbus said. "I'm going to have a lie-in. Magic takes it out of you."

"But I did all the flying," Will protested.

"Yes, and who made your wings grow? Tell me that."

Will decided that Nimbus had a point.

"I'll be here about half past ten."

"Perfect," Nimbus said, "and get your Gran to make some extra sandwiches. I like crumbly cheese on white bread with a few sliced gherkins. Oh, and ask her if she can pack you some homemade cakes or scones. I'm partial to a slice of cake."

"See you in the morning," Will said.

"See you then."

Will realised the light was fading fast. He scooped up his rucksack. The wings were still there so he couldn't put it on yet. One last time he took to the air and glided over the water meadow and across Farmer Sutch's field. By the time he had got to the far side he was finding it harder to stay up. The wings were shrinking. He dropped to the ground, reached back to feel and sure enough, they were gone just as Nimbus had predicted. As he crossed the rickety bridge he slipped the rucksack over his shoulders. Halfway down Owl Heart Lane he saw a fast moving shape in the sky. It was an owl. He wondered if it was the one he had seen outside his window. Then the light came in his grandparents' living room window.

He started to run.

Chapter Seven
Pictures on the wall

He turned into the drive and saw that Granddad was cutting the hedge. He was using a pair of shears with wooden handles.

"Why don't you buy a pair of hedgeclippers?" Will asked. "That's what Dad uses. They run on electricity. I'm sure it would be much easier."

"I've got a pair of good, strong hands," Granddad said. "I don't see the point of wasting electricity."

Will could see his point.

"Isn't it hard work though?"

"Of course it's hard work. That's the point. It keeps you fit and strong. If everything in life is easy you get fat and sluggish." Granddad paused and wiped the sweat from his brow.

"What have you been doing with yourself this fine, sunny day?"

"Oh, just exploring. I must have walked miles."

"It'll do you good. That's what a boy should be doing, rambling the fields and woods, not sitting staring at the goggle box or blowing things up on a computer."

"You don't have a computer," Will pointed out, "and the TV here only has four channels."

"That's all we need," Granddad said. "Besides, we prefer to read a book in the evening."

"Isn't that a bit boring?" Will asked.

"That depends on the book," Granddad said. "What kind of book do you like?"

"Adventure books."

"Anything else?"

"Football books."

"Anything else?"

"Well, I have always wanted to find a wizard's spell book. That would be so cool."

"You might find one some day," Granddad said.

"I don't think so," Will said.

"Oh, you never know."

"Choose a book for me," Will said.

"Very well, I will." Granddad glanced at Will's rucksack. "Did you eat your packed lunch?"

"Yes, I ate all the sandwiches and the flapjack. I drank all the orange juice too. I even ate the apple and pear."

"Fruit's good for you. Don't you forget it."

"I won't."

Will turned to go.

"Oh, Will."

"Yes, Granddad?"

"Tell your Gran to make you a bigger packed lunch in the morning. You're a growing boy."

Will saw a kind of twinkle in Granddad's eyes. Did he know something?

"OK, I will," he said.

Gran was making the tea when Will opened the door.

"What are we having?" he asked.

"Are you hungry?"

"Starving," Will said. "Granddad says you should make me a bigger packed lunch tomorrow."

Gran smiled.

"Then I will. Would you like anything special in it?"

"Yes," Will said, remembering what Nimbus said. "Can I have some sandwiches made with crusty, white bread and crumbly cheese and sliced gherkins and a slice of cake and a scone?"

"You know your mind," Gran said. "That's a real country boy's lunch. That's the kind of thing Granddad used to take to work when I first met him."

"Where did Granddad work?"

"He did some labouring for Farmer Sutch and the other farmers hereabouts."

Will remembered that he still didn't know what was for tea.

"So what are we having?"

"A nice chicken and vegetable stew."

Will's stomach was rumbling.

"What's in it?"

"Chicken legs, bacon, celery, mushrooms, leaks, carrots and new potatoes. There's some thyme and black pepper and a good dash of cider to give it flavour."

"It sounds good. How long will it be?"

"Oh, about half an hour. It will give you time to have a bath and wash off all that muck."

"Am I dirty?"

"You look like a chimney sweep. You may as well get into your pyjamas. You won't be going out again."

Will had his bath and dressed in his pyjamas. While he was waiting for tea to be ready, he wandered round the cottage looking at the pictures on the walls. It was the first time he had ever examined them properly. He had visited his grandparents' cottage many times, but it was the first time he had paid close attention to the pictures.

There were the recent ones in colour, though even some of them must have been taken some years ago. The colour in a few of them was fading, as if the people were going to vanish completely. Then there were the black and white photos. Even older were the sepia brown ones. Older still were the paintings of village scenes.

"These pictures go back to the olden days, don't they Gran?"

Gran came into the living room wiping her hands on a tea towel.

"The paintings go back hundreds of years."

"So the family has lived in Greengate for a long time?"

"Yes, we've been here as long as anyone can remember, my side of the family and your Granddad's side. Your Mum is the first person to move away. Maybe that's half the trouble."

She looked sad for a moment then perked up.

Will pointed at a man with a long, white beard. He was sitting in the middle of a crowd of men, women and children of various ages.

"Who's he?"

"That's my Granddad."

"He reminds me of somebody," Will said.

Then he had it. Great Great Granddad looked a bit like Nimbus

with his flowing, white beard. He was much taller of course.

"Tell me about the people in the pictures," Will said.

Gran talked about the scenes of village life. She told him about harvest time and Christmas, Easter and Oak Apple Day, May Day and All Saints Day. She told him about the carnivals and dances they used to have.

"There isn't so much of that kind of thing any more," she said sadly. "People prefer to sit watching their TVs. Besides, there are lots of newcomers to the village living here now."

Will peered at one of the photos.

"Why is there a monkey on the wall of that house?"

"That's Monkey Lodge. I'll take you to see it some time. That's enough questions for now. Tea's ready."

Chapter Eight
The second wish

Next morning Will was out of the house on the stroke of ten. He could hear the church bell chiming as he set off. His rucksack was heavier than it had been the day before. Gran had made him extra sandwiches and plenty of slices of cake and scones. There was a big, plastic bottle of apple juice and lots of fruit. It wasn't going to take him half an hour to reach the thicket, but he was too impatient to spend any more time hanging round the house. Halfway down Owl Heart Lane he paused to gaze at the ominous storm clouds. They were deep violet and they were getting darker.

"Please don't rain," he said out loud.

He wanted the day to stay fine so he could have new adventures. He still couldn't decide what to wish for. He didn't want to ask for something stupid like money. It would only vanish at the end of the day. Maybe he should ask if he could go somewhere special, like the plains of Africa or the snows of the Arctic. Imagine if he could wish for a spell book of his very own, but he knew that would be breaking the rules. Nimbus said one spell at a time.

"Imagine if I could become a wizard," he said, knowing there was nobody around to wonder who he was talking to. "Then things would get really interesting."

He remembered the way Granddad said it wasn't impossible.

Maybe it was true. Greengate was a place where magic was in the air. Will reached the rickety bridge and looked into the racing water. He could see the dark shapes of the minnows, the flash of their scales and the ripple of their fins. He found himself wondering what it would be like to explore that underwater world.

"That's it," he said, snapping his fingers. "I grew wings yesterday. I'll ask if I can grow fins today."

The clouds were even darker by the time he got to Farmer Sutch's field. A few fat drops of rain were splashing on the corn. Suddenly it didn't seem to matter whether it rained or not. He would be getting wet anyway.

Nimbus was waiting for him at the well. He was very still at first, just like the first time when he was able to pass for a little gnome made of pot. As soon as Will made his way into the thicket a broad smile spread across his face.

"Good morning, Will."

Will glanced up at the sky. Raindrops pattered on his cheeks.

"It isn't very good, is it?"

"Try being my size," Nimbus said. "Each raindrop is like a jug of water."

"I never thought of that." Will said.

"Big people never think about little people."

"I've started to," Will said, "now that I know you're real."

"So what will it be?" Nimbus said. "Have you come up with a new wish?"

"I have," Will said. "I want my Mum and Dad to stop arguing. I want things to be like they used to be."

"Sorry Will," Nimbus said. "I can't interfere with the human heart. It is up to your Mum and Dad to sort their own lives out."

Will felt sad for a few moments then he snapped out of it.

"OK, if I can't get Mum and Dad back together, I want to have a spell book and become a wizard."

"Oh, you're not ready for anything like that yet," Nimbus said.

Will was disappointed.

"Then I want to grow fins like a fish and swim in the river."

"That's more like it for a beginner," Nimbus said. "Here, hand me the rucksack. I'll keep it safe and dry for you."

Will handed it over.

"There are crumbly cheese sandwiches on white bread," he said, peering inside. "Did you remember the gherkins?"

"I did."

"What about the cakes and scones?"

"Lots."

"You've done well, young Will," Nimbus said.

"Don't eat them all when I'm away," Will said anxiously.

"As if I could," Nimbus said. "Haven't you noticed how big I am?"

"You could invite your friends round to scoff the lot," Will said.

"Well, I'm not going to," Nimbus said. "That would be very bad manners. Now, do you want me to grant your wish?"

"Yes please. Do I have to take my clothes off?"

"Why would you want to do that?"

"I don't want to get them wet."

"Don't worry. You won't."

"But I'll be underwater," Will said.

"It's magic, Will. You won't get wet."

Nimbus unscrewed his fishing rod and made the passes with his wand.

"My legs feel funny," Will said.

"You'd better hurry down to the river while you've still got legs rather than a tail fin."

"You mean I'm going to look like a merman...er...merboy?"

"Exactly."

Will scampered off towards the river. He hadn't gone far when he thought of something.

"Don't you need to teach me how to swim underwater?"

"You can swim, can't you?" Nimbus asked.

"Of course I can. I'm a good swimmer. I came second in the gala."

"Just do what you usually do. It's much easier than flying."

Will was glad to hear it. That branch had really hurt his head. By the time he reached the riverbank it was getting hard to move. His legs were sticking together and scales were growing over his skin. He struggled to the very edge and dived in with a splash.

Chapter Nine
Hooked

Nimbus was right. It was much easier than flying. At first he used his arms to swim, but he soon realised he could just let them trail by his side. His powerful tail fin did all the work. It was easily strong enough to propel him down the river. He didn't have to worry about breathing underwater either. It was just like breathing air.

He plunged deeper and deeper until he was skimming the muddy bottom of the river. Startled fish scattered as he went faster and faster, knifing through the water.

He rolled over so he was gliding through the depths, gazing up at the rippling sunlight. A pike came by and considered him for a moment before vanishing with a flick of its tail. This is so cool, Will thought. Was it better than flying? He wasn't sure. It gave him the same sense of freedom. He was about to turn and swim back the way he came when there was a sudden tug.

Will frowned. What was that? There it was again, a sharp, hard tug. He tried to continue on his way, but something was holding him back. He twisted and turned, trying to work out what was wrong. That's when he saw the reason for his difficulty. The barb of a fishing hook had snagged his trousers. The line pulled tight. It was dragging him up to the surface by his bottom. Will panicked. He reached round, trying to free himself. Then, just as he was reaching out for the hook, there was another powerful tug. A fisherman was reeling him in.

No matter how Will wriggled and squirmed, kicked and fought, the line was dragging him ever closer to the surface. Soon he was able to see the bending fishing rod and the wavy shadow of the angler. I can't let him see me, Will thought, but what could he do? Every time he reached for the hook and line, the angler would reel him in even harder. He was just too strong.

Finally, the fisherman managed to reel Will to the surface. Will gazed up, startled, but he was nowhere near as startled as the man on the riverbank. He gaped at the boy dangling on the end of his line. Will stared back.

"You're….a boy!" the angler said.

The funniest idea came into Will's head. He decided to tough it out.

"No, I'm not," he said. "I'm a fish."

"I know what a fish looks like," the angler said, "and you're no fish."

"I've got a tail fin," Will said stubbornly. "Explain that."

The angler looked stumped.

"See, you can't."

"You're not a fish," the angler said finally.

"Yes, I am."

"No, you're not."

"So what am I?" Will demanded.

"You're a... you're a...you're a merman...merboy," the angler stammered.

Will finally wriggled free of the the hook and dived back into the river. He swam as fast as he could back to the spot where he had dived in. He dragged himself onto the bank and glanced back. The angler was running along the riverbank towards him. Will tried to run, but it was hard now that his legs had been turned into a tail fin. All he could do was waddle.

"Come back!" the angler yelled. "You're going to make me famous, merboy. It will be like catching the Loch Ness monster."

Will thought it was nothing like catching the Loch Ness monster. His heart was pounding. The angler couldn't catch him. It would ruin everything. He was waddling as fast as he could, but it was so hard. He kept falling flat on his face. The angler was getting closer. Will tried hopping the way he had in the sack race at school. This was better than waddling, but not much. Still, the angler was gaining. Just when it seemed certain that he was going to get caught, his tail fin vanished and he was able to run. He sprinted away as fast as his freed legs could carry him. He had soon left the angler far behind. He scrambled into the thicket and lay on his tummy, holding his breath. He heard the angler's boots on the ground nearby. The man cursed.

"Where are you, merboy?"

Will pressed himself to the ground.

"I know you're there."

The angler was beating the bushes with his rod.

"Merboy!"

Will felt the rod swish past his left ear. The search went on for several minutes then the angler stamped away, disappointed. After a few moments Will peeked through the branches and saw him disappearing in the distance.

"That was a close call," came a voice.

"Nimbus!"

"Who do you think magicked your tail fin back into legs?"

"Thank you," Will said.

"Any time," Nimbus said.

He scratched his head.

"We need to be a bit more careful," Nimbus said. "We can't have some human catching you."

"I wouldn't tell them about you," Will said.

"They might force you."

"Cross my heart," Will said. "They would never force it out of me. Never!"

His eyes were stinging.

"Don't cry," Nimbus said.

"I'm not!" Will protested.

He nearly was, of course, but he didn't want to show himself up in front of the gnome.

"I'm glad to hear it," Nimbus said. "He didn't catch you so there's no harm done."

Will cheered up. Nimbus grinned and vanished into the thicket. He returned a few moments later, dragging the rucksack.

"Time for lunch."

Chapter Ten
Lunch with a gnome...and a chase

Now Nimbus couldn't eat a whole cheese sandwich, though he did his very best, but he could manage a small chunk of crusty bread, a fat crumb of cheese and a small slice of gherkin.

"You've got a very good appetite," Will said, "for a gnome."

"I've got a very good appetite," Nimbus said, "for a horse!"

That made Will laugh. He watched as Nimbus set about a nugget of lemon drizzle cake and a small chunk of scone with a smear of butter and agreed that, yes, Nimbus really could eat like a horse.

"A horse with a beard," Will chuckled.

"A horse with a beard and a very fat, round tummy," Nimbus added.

"Would you like some fruit?" Will asked. "Gran says it's good for you."

"If I ate another morsel," Nimbus grunted, "it would be very bad for me. I would explode. There would be little lumps of gnome dangling from the trees."

"That sounds messy," Will observed.

"Very," Nimbus said. "Gnomes aren't meant to explode."

Will changed the subject.

"Do you think that angler will tell everybody about the merboy he caught?"

"Let him," Nimbus said. "Nobody will believe him."

"He seemed pretty determined," Will said. "He chased me all the way from the river."

"Don't worry about your fisherman friend," Nimbus said. "He's just a windbag. If he starts talking about boys with fishes' tails everybody will be thinking he's been knocking back the cider."

"Are you sure?"

"I'm positive."

This time it was Nimbus who changed the subject.

"How was your underwater adventure?"

"It was pretty good," Will said, "until I got hooked."

"I bet he thought he'd caught a big one," Nimbus said. "I wish I could have seen the look on his face."

"He did look shocked," Will said.

They were still laughing at the thought of the bewildered angler staring at a merboy dangling by the seat of his pants when Will heard something.

"What's that?"

Nimbus frowned.

"Something wrong?"

"Listen."

It was the sound of barking and it was coming closer. Nimbus scrambled to the thicket opening.

"Dogs! It's that angler. He's come back with a couple of dogs."

"I told you he was determined," Will said. "What are we going to do?"

"You've got to put the dog off the scent," Nimbus said. "Dogs and gnomes don't mix. That nosy fisherman mustn't find me."

"I've got an idea," Will said. "Can I have more than one wish in a day?"

"You can have as many as you like," Nimbus told him. "But only one at a time and don't forget, the moment the light dies, the wish dies with it."

Will whispered in Nimbus' ear.

48

"You really are the most remarkable boy," Nimbus said. "That's a brilliant idea."

Nimbus waved his wand and the transformation began. Will's top lip twitched and tingled. Whiskers sprouted. His bottom prickled and soon a tail grew. Fur spread over his skin.

"Right," Nimbus said, scrambling up the side of the well. "You're all set. Time to put your plan into action."

Will didn't need any more encouragement. He could see the angler coming closer with his dogs.

"If there is something more interesting to a dog than a gnome," Will whispered to Nimbus who was now crouching on top of the well, "it's a….cat!"

With that, he burst from the thicket and set off towards Farmer Sutch's field. Of course, the dogs didn't see a boy. They saw a cat. They took off after him, baying at the top of their voices. The angler waddled along behind, puffing and panting. He was rather a fat fisherman. Will's paws flew across the grass. He could hear the dogs behind him. You're in for a shock, he thought. Once he got the dogs well away from the thicket, he would spring his surprise.

The dogs were gaining. By now they were going crazy, yelping and snarling, sure that they were going to catch him.

"That's right," Will whispered to himself. "Keep on coming. Closer, closer, now!"

Turning into a cat was only the beginning. Now it was time for the second part of the spell. He squirmed through a gap in the hedge, knowing the angler could no longer see him. Will led the dogs into Farmer Sutch's field.

"You've been chasing a small cat. Now you're going to catch a *big* one."

With that, he spun round, transforming into a great, tawny lion. He planted his paws and gave a thunderous roar. Instantly, the

dogs turned tail in panic. They cannoned into the oncoming angler and left him sprawling on the ground.

"What's got into you?" he shouted after the retreating dogs. "It's only a little pussy cat."

He was still watching his fleeing dogs when Will came up behind him. The angler froze, feeling hot breath on the back of his neck. Will raised a paw and tapped him on the shoulder. Slowly, barely daring to breathe, the angler turned....and screamed.

"Lion!"

Then he ran off in the opposite direction as fast as his fat, little legs could carry him. Will gave another loud roar. Nimbus poked his head out of the thicket and nodded. He waved his wand and Will turned back into a nine-year-old boy. Something told him the angler would think twice about returning to the thicket, but that wasn't the end of the story.

Will and Nimbus were heading into much bigger trouble.

Chapter Eleven
Imps!

Next morning Will set off about ten o'clock just as he had the day before. It was a warm, dry summer's morning so he strode along happily trying to make his mind up what to wish for. He had had a go at flying and swimming underwater. Nimbus said he wasn't ready to have his own spell book. Maybe he should turn himself into a giant or a tiny, little person like Tom Thumb. He was still turning these things over in his mind when he arrived at the thicket. He made his way through the tangle of branches to the well and discovered Nimbus hopping up and down tugging at his hair in despair.

"Whatever is the matter?" Will asked.

"I only dozed off for a minute," Nimbus said. "I swear. It was just a minute."

Will wasn't sure what to say. Why did falling asleep matter so much? Everybody did it. Granddad fell asleep in his armchair every evening.

"What am I going to do?" Nimbus said. "Whatever am I going to do?"

"Maybe you should tell me what's wrong," Will suggested.

"They got out," Nimbus cried. "Don't you understand? They got out and now there is going to be terrible trouble."

"Nimbus," Will said, "you have got to calm down. *Who* got out?"

"The imps! Half a dozen of them must have escaped before I

woke up and slammed the lid down to stop the rest getting out."

Will glanced at the well.

"So it isn't just a wishing well?"

Nimbus stared at him as if he had said too much.

"Nimbus?"

"It's not just a wishing well," Nimbus admitted.

"I think you had better explain."

Nimbus sat cross-legged on the board covering the well.

"Long, long ago when towns were few and carts trundled between the villages on dirt tracks there were all kinds of woodland folk. There were witches and warlocks and gnomes and goblins and brownies and...."

"Imps?"

"Quite. Now some woodland folk, the gnomes and fairy people, they wanted to live in peace alongside you humans."

"Something tells me that wasn't true of all the woodland folk,"

Will said.

Nimbus shook his head.

"No," he said. "Some of them thought the human tribe was taking over, pushing the woodland folk out of their homes."

Will thought of the roads and towns and cities and all the traffic and noise and pollution.

"They might have had a point."

"They did," Nimbus agreed, "but what were we to do about it? If we started a war the humans would destroy us. There is no creature more warlike than a human. It had to be better to live alongside them."

"It kind of makes sense."

"It makes perfect sense. If I were to challenge a human to a fight, even a small human like you, the human could squash me under his boot."

"But surely you could use magic to fight the humans," Will said.

"Oh no, oh no, no, no, I couldn't do that. I'm not allowed to use magic to hurt anyone."

"So what are the wishing wells for if they are not just for granting wishes?"

Nimbus owned up. He patted the brick wall of the well.

"This didn't start out as a wishing well at all, Will Antrobus. It was a gateway between the mischievous folk in the world below and the human world above. Gnomes and fairies and the like gave up living in the underworld. We preferred to live in the light alongside you humans. Now, imps and goblins and witches and warlocks, they live down there and they only come out to do mischief. When they come out of the dark they bring some of the dark with them."

"Go on," Will said, curious to know how the wishes fitted in to all this.

"It's like this," Nimbus said. "Most humans are too preoccupied with the ups and downs of their own lives to even notice the woodland folk that mean them no harm. Some of them walk right past me without noticing I am even here. The woodland folk they notice are the wicked ones. My job is to stop them escaping from the underworld. That way I can keep the peace between my kind and yours."

"So you're a kind of guardian?"

"I am indeed," Nimbus said proudly, puffing out his chest. "We gnomes guard the openings between the underworld and the overworld. We seal the wells with our magic boards."

Will stared at the board.

"What's magic about a greasy, rotting piece of wood?"

"It might look like a greasy, rotting piece of wood to you," Nimbus said, "but that is a disguise. No creature of the underworld can move the board while I stand guard over the well."

"But you didn't stand guard," Will reminded him. "You fell asleep."

"I know," Nimbus wailed, "and that's how the imps got out."

"So why do you grant me wishes?"

"Isn't it obvious?" Nimbus cried.

"No, not really."

"I can't leave the well,"Nimbus explained. "That's why I have to find a three-seer like you. If I can find a child, a special child who doesn't walk by when he sees a gnome, I can grant him wishes that give him the power to capture any escaped mischief-makers."

"Oh, I get it!"

Nimbus sighed.

"At last."

"So I've got to get the imps back?"

"Got it in one."

"How do I do that?" Will asked. "What wish should I ask for?"

"I have no idea," Nimbus said. "We've got to come up with a plan."

So they sat on the edge of the well and tried to think up a plan that would return the imps to the underworld.

Chapter Twelve
The plan

While Will and Nimbus were thinking, the imps were up to mischief. They gave Greengate a miss and went after a much bigger prize, the nearby town of Westwich. Half a dozen imps can travel fast. An imp is small, no bigger than a handspan, so half the size of a gnome, but ferociously nimble and fast. It is not as nasty as the notoriously malevolent goblin, but it loves nothing better than to see some poor, unfortunate human reduced to tears of despair by one of its pranks.

The imps entered Westwich about eleven o'clock in the morning on the back of a builder's flat back truck.

"It's market day," the leader Pricklepot said, rubbing his bony hands with glee. "That means it will be busy. Lots of people to tease."

The imps' first victim was a postman called Terry Smith. Now there is nothing a postman fears more than a fierce dog and the imps knew this very well. While a pair of lookout imps followed Terry on his round, the other four scurried off round the town looking for the fiercest dogs they could find. Whenever they tracked down a suitably grumpy hound, they would whisper their plan into its ear in fluent Barksnuffle, which is the commonest of the canine languages.

The first dog they recruited was a fearsome bloodhound called Bayleaf. The second was an aristocratic Alsatian called Albrecht.

They soon added a Jack Russell terrier who, surprisingly enough, was called Jack, a Dachshund called Dash and a rather unhinged Mastiff by the name of Lockjaw. Once they had assembled their pack of four-legged tormentors, they went looking for Terry. An impish whistle helped them locate him halfway down Mill Lane. Terry was bending down, struggling to squeeze a small package through the letterbox, when he heard a low growl behind him. He stiffened. Then there was a snarl to his left followed by another one to his right. Slowly, cautiously, he straightened up and took in the dreadful sight of a quartet of savage mutts surrounding him. From somewhere he heard the sound of gleeful laughter, but he couldn't see who was making that awful, cackling noise.

He decided to make a fun for it. Moments later, Terry was sprinting off down the street pursued by the dogs. The pack was under strict instructions not to bite, but to give Terry the fright of his life. Of course, poor Terry wasn't to know that. Any moment he expected the nearest mutt to sink its teeth into the seat of his pants. Were the imps satisfied with their prank? Not a bit of it! It only gave Pricklepot a taste for more.

"What next?" he wondered.

That's when he spotted the fat, grey and white herring gulls wheeling overhead.

"The very thing," he said. "A dive bomber."

"With a full load," another of the imps added.

As any driver will know, herring gulls are not fussy where they do their business. Many a morning some poor car owner will come out of his or her front door and groan at the sight of the white splashes on their precious vehicles. That's right, they've been bird-pooped. The imps made a pyramid of bodies so that Pricklepot could make himself heard over the wind.

"I say, you lords of the air," he called, shamelessly flattering the gulls. "Would you like to join in our game?"

He was speaking Featherfriend, the commonest of the bird languages. As you can see, imps are great learners of languages. He explained his plan and the gulls agreed to their part without hesitation. Soon there was mayhem in the town. The gulls spattered the pavements and bombarded the cars. They peppered the windows and splatted every hat. They even targeted the children's ice creams! How the imps giggled to see the crowds fleeing into shops and pubs, doorways and bus shelters to escape the swooping birds. But was Pricklepot satisfied? He was not.

"It's lunchtime," he said. "We will have something to eat then we'll pick up where we left off. It will lull them into a false sense of security."

The imps agreed to the plan and went in search of food. They discovered the back door to a café and slipped inside. The cook didn't notice them watching from the corner of the fridge.

"Fish, chips and peas, pie and mash and a spaghetti bolognese," the waitress said.

The cook, whose name was Charlie, prepared the meals and shouted the waitress. He only took his eye off the plates for a moment, but that was enough for the imps.

"Service," the cook shouted.

Sally the waitress arrived and planted her hands on her hips.

"Is this some kind of joke?" she demanded.

Charlie couldn't believe his eyes. The fish was gone and most of the chips. The pie was half eaten and there were strands of spaghetti everywhere. That wasn't the only thing puzzling him. What was that strange cackling sound coming from the yard outside? Charlie prepared three more meals. This time he watched them like a hawk.

"That's better," Sally said. "Fancy you eating the customers' dinners. You're going barmy, you are."

"It wasn't me," Charlie protested.

"So who was it?" Sally asked. "The little people?"

She didn't know how close she was to the truth.

Chapter Thirteen
Mischief on a full stomach

The imps enjoyed their feast. They crowded round the battered fish and nibbled their way towards the middle until all that was left was one juicy, white morsel in the middle and Pricklepot made light work of that. They then set about the spaghetti. For a while they sucked great lengths of it into their mouths. When they got bored they used the spaghetti as a skipping rope and threw the tomatoey strands at one another. They even made lassoos and tried to rope one another, but the spaghetti always snapped.

Finally they turned to their favourite, the pie. They gathered stones and bricks and iced lolly sticks and made springboards. They formed a circle and they all dived into the piping hot pie at once, slurping the gravy and gobbling down chunks of meat and potato. They then crawled off into a corner where they wouldn't be seen and slept off the meal. They woke up an hour or so later and heard the town hall clock chime three.

"Three o'clock," Pricklepot said. "You know what that means."

"Nearly four o'clock?" a particularly stupid imp called Windnoggin suggested.

Pricklepot slapped him across his bald, bumpy head.

"Don't be such a thick, clunking dumbskull," Pricklepot scolded. "It's the best time of day for an imp. Think of school."

"Hometime!" the other imps cried in unison.

"Exactly," Pricklepot said. "Just imagine the fun we can have with all those kiddlywinks. They squeal and run even more than the grown ups do. Let's go."

And go they did. They soon reached Westwich County Primary School and perched on a wall opposite the main gate. It wasn't long before the bell rang and the children came racing out of the building. The imps got to work. They pelted the children with mud and dirt. They tied the girls' ponytails together. They pushed the boys into puddles. They grabbed school bags and lunch boxes. All in all, they had a whale of a time and they didn't even have to go in the water. Best of all, they were so quick nobody had any idea what was causing the mayhem.

The head teacher, Mrs Gwendolen Wiffleton-Scrommit, came out to see what all the fuss was about. Pricklepot took a good look at her and decided she was the perfect target for his latest prank. While Mrs Wiffleton-Scrommit was trying to calm the children and reassure the parents, Pricklepot whispered orders to his fellow imps. They went quick as a flash and returned with two huge tubs of bright green fence paint from the Do It Yourself store and a trolley full of other goodies. Pricklepot organised his imps into two groups. They climbed onto the tall gateposts at the school entrance, dragging the paint tubs after them. Once they had got the tubs balanced on the gateposts, they eased off the lids. Pricklepot arranged the tubs so they were just above Mrs Wiffleton-Scrommit's head and started to count

"Ten, nine, eight...."

Mrs Wiffleton-Scrommit frowned. Was that a tiny voice she had just heard?

"Seven, six, five....."

Where was it coming from?

"Four, three, two...."

"Mrs Wiffleton-Scrommit," one of the parents cried, seeing the tubs perched precariously on the gateposts.

Mrs Wiffleton-Scrommit looked up, but it was too late to avert disaster.

"One!" Pricklepot cried.

Down came the tubs and with a huge *glump* the green paint came down on Mrs Wiffleton-Scrommit's head. A moment later she looked like a giant gooseberry and a giant, wailing gooseberry at that, because she was howling at the top of her voice. Now, it was bad enough for the unfortunate Mrs Wiffleton-Scrommit that she was drenched in bright emerald green paint, but it was even worse that she couldn't see the culprits who did it. The imps were simply too fast, too cunning, too clever for any of their human victims. There was nobody to blame, nobody to punish.

"Who is responsible?" the head teacher shrieked.

"Who is to blame?" the staring crowd demanded.

"What's going on?" the children cried.

Nobody had an answer, nobody but the imps and they were rolling round on the lawn just beyond a nearby garden wall, thoroughly enjoying the chaotic scene. Before long, PC Harry Futtock, the local bobby, turned up on his bike.

"Now then, now then," he said, because policemen always say things twice, "what's going on here then?"

The villagers' answers to his question soon filled ten pages of his notebook. He took off his helmet and scratched his head.

"This is most peculiar, most, most peculiar."

One by one, the imps peered over the garden wall. Their bright, mischievous eyes lighted on the policeman. PC Harry Futtock was now a marked man.

"Put your thinking caps on," Pricklepot said. "We need something extra special for PC Futtock."

"A kick up the buttock?" Windnoggin said.

"A kick up the buttock for PC Futtock?" Pricklepot sneered. "That's just the kind of brainless suggestion I would expect from you, Windnoggin."

Then he spotted something round the back of the house. He had an idea.

"Got it," said Pricklepot. "Get jam."

The other imps exchanged bewildered glances. Whatever could Pricklepot want with jam?

"Oh, and something to play music."

The imps were more confused than ever. Why did he want to play music?

Chapter Fourteen
Getting a buzz from your job

If the crowd had stopped shouting for a moment they might have heard the sound of locks being prised off garden sheds. They might have noticed the noise of sawing and hammering, the tightening of screws and the stretching of rubber inner tubes. They might have become aware of the clink of glass jars and the loud gloop of strawberry and raspberry jam oozing from their necks and landing –splat– in large wooden scoops fashioned by the imps. They might have even heard Pricklepot issue the order for the imps to get out their Walpurgis whistles. What's a Walpurgis whistle, you ask. Read on and you will find out.

"Blow!" Pricklepot ordered.

The imps blew and from their Walpurgis whistles came the eeriest sound you have ever heard. It wasn't loud, but such was its pitch that the villagers immediately stopped yelling and arguing.

"What's that?" they asked each other.

"It's the sound of flutes," one man said.

"No," the woman next to him insisted, "it reminds me of an Australian didgeridoo. Can't you hear the buzz at the end?"

The buzz, of course, was the clue to the Walpurgis whistle's strange power. It could summon all kinds of creatures to commit mischief. The Walpurgis whistle is one of the most important weapons in the woodland folk's armoury. It begins with a long, sad note that alerts wild creatures to the presence of an imp or goblin, brownie or sprite. Then the note mimics the sound of the creature summoned, in this case every bee, wasp or hornet for miles around. They could hear it calling them in their own language. It is called Fizzledebizz. Where did Pricklepot get the idea for his latest wheeze? Why, from the beehive in the back garden of the house where the imps were hiding.

It wasn't long before the drone of insects filled the air.

"Do you hear that?" one small girl asked, gazing at the sky.

"I don't like the sound of it at all," her mother said, squeezing the child's chubby hand tightly.

That's when Pricklepot gave the order.

"Prime the catapults."

The imps tugged the levers that turned the gears that tightened the rubber inner tubes. They built up the tension that had the wooden scoops full of jam quivering.

"Fire the catapults!"

The imps released the triggers that launched the jam that flew through the air and showered the teachers and parents, children and tots and, right at the very centre of the crowd, taking the biggest hit, PC Harry Futtock.

"Now blow on your whistles. Signal the attack!"

The sky turned black with swarms of bees, wasps and hornets. They formed into dart-like formations. Pricklepot chose the piece of music he wanted. Ride of the Valkyries blasted from the speaker.

"Led the mayhem commence!"

Black and orange menace plunged from the sky. The crowd scattered. The lucky ones scrambled into the school building. Others locked themselves in cars. Still others dived into the town pond. They were the lucky ones. Poor PC Futtock and a few unlucky parents were soon fleeing down Market Street pursued by dense swarms of insects.

"What next?" Windnoggin asked, clapping his hands with glee.

"Mm," Pricklepot said. "What next indeed?"

That's when he heard a loud roar.

"What's that?" he asked. "Windnoggin, shimmy up that lamp post and see what you can see?"

What Windnoggin saw was Westwich Victoria scoring the first goal in the Fartington and Trumpwell Baked Beans Premier League.

"It's a football match," he shouted.

Pricklepot slapped his forehead.

"A football match! Why, that's perfect. Are there many people there?"

Windnoggin started to count.

"One, two, three…"

"I don't want you to count every person, you pimplebrain," Pricklepot scolded. "Just give me a rough idea."

"I would say there are a few thousand," Windnoggin said.

"A few thousand!"

Pricklepot slapped his scrawny thigh and his eyes lit up.

"Oh, that is a written invitation to an imp. Let's go."

Chapter Fifteen
Match of the day

At that very moment Will got off the bus about five minutes' walk from the Victoria Ground. He was carrying a large net. For reasons that will become clear later he didn't have to pay the fare. He heard a loud roar from the stadium.

"Goal!"

Button Albion's marking on the corner was dreadful. Recently signed Westwich striker Fernando Castanets slipped behind Albion defender Zack Wobbly to volley the ball into the net. He peeled away, arms outstretched, golden hair flowing in the breeze, Alice band sparkling like a tiara and basked in the applause from the fans at the Greengate End. Chants of 'Nando, Nando' echoed round the ground.

Will listened for a moment then walked on. He had no idea that's where the imps were headed. Why would he? While Will roamed the streets of Westwich, searching for some sign of the imps, his quarry was scampering unseen down the players' tunnel. The imps were headed for the changing rooms. Paint wasn't the only thing they had lifted from the DIY store.

Just before half time it was all Abion. Midfield general Tommy Haddock was pulling the strings. He sprayed the ball out to Andy Lipsalve, Albion's nippy, young winger. Lipsalve crossed into the box. Muscular centre forward Kyle Headbanger met it and sent it thumping into the back of the net beyond the despairing fingers of Darren Porous, the Vics' goalie. 1-1. Will heard that shout too, but still he didn't realise that's where he would find the escaped imps.

"Where are they?" he groaned.

It was at that moment he spotted PC Futtock pounding down the High Street pursued by a swarm of chasing bees, wasps and hornets. Will leapt into action, brandishing his net. With one swipe of the net he caught most of the insects. Unaware of what had just happened, PC Futtock carried on his way. Will planted the open end of the net on the ground and waited for the insects' anger to subside. Once they had stopped their angry buzzing, he freed them. Will was quite pleased with what he had done, but the policeman had vanished. Will knew the imps were behind this, but where could they be?

Back at the Victoria Ground the ref whistled for half time and the players headed down the tunnel. In the home changing room Vics captain Mick McMuck flopped down.

"Odd," he grunted.

He couldn't get back up. He was stuck to the bench. It was the same story in the Albion changing room where full back Sean Hare discovered the imps' little joke.

"Don't sit down. There's superglue on the bench."

It was too late. The whole team was stuck. Five minutes later the Vics manager Norm Gorm came rushing up to referee Joshua Limbo.

"We need to delay kick-off."

He explained that there weren't enough shorts to replace the ones glued to the bench. Somebody had gone out to the shops. Two minutes later Albion Manager Arthur Mo turned up with a similar story. The tannoy explained to the fans that the second half would be starting ten minutes late. When the teams finally took to the pitch there was much whistling and even more laughter. Some were wearing football shorts, but there hadn't been enough to go round. Others were wearing brightly coloured Bermuda shorts. Some even had to wear orange and pink ones. The imps weren't finished. In fact, they hadn't even started. Sean Hare brought Fernando Castanets down in the penalty area. "Penalty!" the crowd roared.

The ref pointed to the spot. Castanets took a short run up and struck the ball confidently. It flew past the outstretched hands of the Albion keeper but, just as the Vics' fans were about to celebrate the goal, it inexplicably bounced out again. Nobody had seen Pricklepot jump out from behind the right hand post and head it out. Castanets stared in disbelief.

Andy Lipsalve picked up the ball from the freekick, beat two men and prepared to unleash a fierce shot at goal. When he swung his right foot it swept his standing left foot off the turf and sent him crashing to the ground. The Vics fans roared with

laughter. Mick McMuck leapt on the loose ball, but he too tumbled to the ground. To his astonishment his laces were tied together.

Elsewhere, Will was starting to despair of finding the imps. He was moving from street to street, eavesdropping on conversations, when he heard an elderly gentleman say something really interesting.

"Did you hear what the commentator said on the radio?" he asked the man next to him. "All kinds of strange things are going on down at the Vics' ground."

That was all Will needed to hear.

"Which way is the ground?" he asked.

The two men stared in disbelief.

"Who said that?" the elderly gentleman asked.

Will felt stupid. How could he have forgotten what he had wished back at the thicket? Nimbus had made him invisible. Leaving the men still wondering about the voice that had just come out of thin air, Will raced towards the Victoria Ground. Inside things were going from bad to worse. Water bottles sprayed the substitutes. Meat pies smacked into faces. The imps were having a whale of a time. Finally, Will arrived, ducking under the nearest turnstile. By then, the whole stadium was erupting in mayhem. People were running for the exit. Players were sprawling everywhere. It was time to act.

Will spotted his first imp picking pockets a few rows from where he was standing. With one sweep of the net he had him. He gathered two more by the dugout where they were puncturing all the footballs. Windnoggin was an easy capture. He just stood by the corner flag while the net scooped him up. But where was Pricklepot? Will tied the struggling imps hand and feet and started searching for any more signs of chaos.

There were screams and shouts from the club restaurant and Will instantly knew who was responsible. He saw the staff sheltering behind upturned tables while sausages and pasties, baked beans and prawn sandwiches, baguettes and buns, curry and kebabs showered them. Will crept unseen towards Pricklepot. The other imps started to yell warnings but it was too late. With one last swish of the net he had Pricklepot in his grasp.

"Time to put you back in the well," Will said.

"Who are you, invisible boy?" Pricklepot squealed.

"Wouldn't you like to know?" Will answered.

Chapter Sixteen
Will does well

Will emptied the imps into the well. He listened to the satisfying splash as they hit the dark waters at the bottom of the well, then the sound of the mischief-makers scrambling onto a dry ledge.

"We'll find out who you are, invisible boy," Pricklepot shouted. "You just wait. If we ever get out again, we'll give you trouble, just see if we don't."

"That's the whole point," Nimbus said. "You're not getting out again. This board stays on the well for ever and a day."

"We know you, Nimbus Cloudbeard," Pricklepot yelled back. "You're a dopy, old gnome. You're always dozing off on the job."

"You wish," Nimbus said.

"Yeah, and if we don't get out, maybe somebody worse will. That's right, invisible boy, if you think imps are bad, try goblins or witches or warlocks. You've let them out before, Nimbus Cloudbeard, and you will let them out again."

"Oh, shut up, you bumpy boneheads!" Nimbus snapped, slamming the lid down on the well.

"Aren't you worried?" Will asked, slightly nervous. "They sounded as if they meant it."

"Forget it," Nimbus said. "Imps are full of hot air."

"Are you sure about that?" Will said.

"I'm positive," Nimbus said reassuringly. "Imps are very small creatures with very big mouths. They like to show off."

They sat side by side for a few minutes watching the sun sinking

low over the oak trees.

"There's something I've always wondered," Will said. "When do you sleep?"

"At night, of course," Nimbus said.

"So who watches the well then?"

"That's up to the night shift."

"Who does the night shift?"

"That's my cousin, Cirrus. He's got a very important job, has Cirrus."

"Why's that?" Will asked.

"Well, it's bad if any of the underworld woodland folk escape in daylight," Nimbus said, "but if you let them loose at night, well, let's just say it's even worse."

"I see."

He wasn't sure he did see, but he didn't want to appear stupid.

"You did well, Will," Nimbus said.

"Thank you," Will said. "I was getting worried when I couldn't find those pesky imps."

"I'm not surprised," Nimbus said. "The longer these imps are at large, the crazier they get. Let them loose for a week or more and they're nearly as bad as goblins or witches."

"So they do get out?"

"It happens sometimes."

"When was the last time?" Will asked.

"That would be twenty years ago," Nimbus said.

"When my mum was a little girl."

"That's right," Nimbus said. "It happened when Holly was eleven, two years older than you."

"How do you know my mum's name?" Will asked.

Nimbus looked a little flustered.

"You told me."

Will frowned.

"Did I?" he asked. "I don't remember that."

"Well, you did," Nimbus said. "My mum's called Holly, you said."

"So what's my dad's name?" Will asked.

"You didn't tell me that."

"What happened when the woodland folk escaped last time?"

"They went crazy," Nimbus said. "We nearly lost Greengate altogether."

"That bad?" Will asked, eyes as wide as saucers.

"That bad," Nimbus said. "It was goblins, you see. They make imps look like angels."

Will remembered all the chaos the imps had caused in Westwich and wondered what goblins could do that was worse.

"It must have been very bad indeed."

"It was."

"I'm going to ask Gran and Granddad about it."

"They won't remember," Nimbus said.

"Why not?"

"It's the way of things. Human memory fades fast when it comes to the woodland folk. They have a kind of recall, but they're never quite sure if it's truth or myth, memory or dream."

"Oh."

Will realised the sun had almost set.

"I'd better be on my way. Goodnight, Nimbus."

Nimbus smiled a gnomish smile.

"Goodnight, Will Antrobus."

The owl appeared and followed him all the way home.

Chapter Seventeen
Memories

Gran left the curtains open that night and the darkness trembled outside. There was a lamp out in the garden and it cast an eerie, yellowish light on the trees.

"What did you do with yourself, today?" Granddad asked, looking up from his newspaper.

"Oh, you know. I climbed a few trees, made a den, walked along the river."

"Holly used to spend all day down there, on the other side of Father Sutch's field," Granddad said. "It was a long, long time ago."

Will heard a lot of sadness in Granddad's voice.

"That must have been twenty years ago."

In the kitchen a cup smashed. Gran appeared in the doorway.

"What made you say that?" she asked.

"Oh, I was just thinking," Will said. "Twenty years ago Mum would have been about my age."

He watched his grandparents' exchange glances. It was as if he had jogged their memories. Granddad was the next to speak.

"There was a great storm, I seem to remember."

"That's right," Gran said. "There was a great storm. It did so much damage."

"Like a gale, you mean," Will asked, "or a hurricane?"

Granddad frowned.

"A storm. Yes, there was a storm, but there was something else."

He glanced at Gran.

"There were people in our garden, little people."

Gran stared for a moment then the spell was broken.

"Little people," she chuckled. "Oh, you silly old goat, what next? You'll be telling me you believe in leprechauns."

She rummaged in a kitchen cupboard and cleared up the broken bits of the cup with a dustpan and brush. Meanwhile, Granddad stared out at the garden. He was still there in his armchair, but his mind had travelled back twenty years. He was chasing ghosts, trying to remember what happened the night of the storm.

"Can you remember anything, Granddad?" Will asked.

"Holly was late," Granddad said absent-mindedly. "She was always home by sunset, but that night she was late home. I went out looking for her."

"Where did you find her?"

"I didn't," Granddad said. "I searched for hours and she was nowhere to be seen."

Then his eyelids fluttered.

"What was I talking about?" he asked.

"The night of the storm," Will reminded him. "You said you went looking for Mum, but you couldn't find her."

Granddad caught Will's eyes.

"I must have done though, mustn't I? I mean, she must have come home. She grew up to be your mum."

Still he gazed out at the dark. His mind was reaching out for something that was no longer there.

"Can you remember anything else?" Will asked.

"The windows broke," Granddad said. "That's right, there was a shower of stones. Somebody broke all our windows."

"Did boys do it?" Will asked, even though he knew it wasn't the right answer.

"It must have been boys," Granddad said. "Who else would break all the windows?"

Will decided to jog Granddad's memory.

"Maybe it was the woodland folk."

A smile lit Granddad's face.

"Oh, you've heard the stories, have you?"

"Did you tell Mum the stories of the woodland folk, Grandddad?"

"I didn't need to," Granddad said. "She discovered them for herself, just like you."

"Do you think Mum remembers the night of the storm?" Will asked.

"You'll have to ask her. She's coming down again the day after tomorrow to see you."

"She doesn't want to take me home, does she?"

"Why?" Granddad asked. "Don't you want to go?"

"I don't think I ever want to go home. Greengate feels like home now."

Gran came in at that moment.

"Oh, isn't that nice?" she said. "There we were thinking you would be homesick and you've really settled in. We miss having a youngster around the house, don't we Granddad?"

Granddad nodded.

"A house is an empty place without a child to fill it with laughter and adventures."

"So why is Mum coming again?"

"Just because she has things to sort out with your father, it doesn't mean she doesn't want to see you. She said she would be down from time to time for a few hours to see you were alright."

"Oh, that's all right," Will said, "just so long as she doesn't want to take me home. I like it here."

Gran smiled.

"Greengate weaves quite a spell, doesn't it?"

Will nodded.

"I think it's…magical."

"I'll tell you what's magical," Granddad said. "Gran's home made parkin."

"Parkin? What's that?"

"It's the most delicious soft cake you will ever eat. I make mine out of oatmeal, golden syrup, butter and ginger. Would you like to try some?"

"Yes please."

Gran came back presently with a plate of parkin cut into squares, a jug of milk and three glasses.

"There you go, Will."

Will took a bite.

"Well?"

"I love it," Will said. "It's so rich and sweet."

He took another bite and a gulp of cold milk.

"It's delicious," he said. "Really scrummy."

Gran beamed.

"Your mum used to love my parkin. Why, she would come back

from one of her adventures and clear a whole plate of it."

"May I have another piece?" Will asked.

"Help yourself."

Will stayed up until ten o'clock then went up to bed. He paused in the hall to look at one of the photographs on the wall. It was taken twenty years earlier. There were Gran and Granddad when they were much younger and Mum when she was a little girl. The colour was faded, but Will could tell that the sky was purple and heavy. Maybe it was the night of the storm. Will was about to climb the stairs when something caught his eye. Just for a second, in the corner of the photo, among the trees, he thought he saw a twisted, wicked-looking face. When he looked again, it was gone.

"I must be seeing things," he murmured.

But he wasn't as he was about to find out.

Chapter Eighteen
A wind from the east

Will woke up and saw the curtains fluttering. The windowpanes were rattling and outside the wind was booming. He scrambled into his jeans and polo shirt, pulled on his socks and laced his trainers. He scrubbed at his teeth and raced downstairs for breakfast. Something told him there was a change in the air.

"Isn't it windy?" he said.

"I don't like the east wind," Gran said. "It brings all kinds of badness."

Will sat at the table.

"Where's Granddad?"

"He's gone into Westwich for some things. The wind damaged the fence last night."

She put a plate of bacon, eggs, sausage and tomatoes in front of Will.

"He must have gone early," Will said, munching a round of toast.

"He wanted to be there when the store opened," Gran explained. "You don't want to leave a fence down. You never know what might get in."

"Dogs, you mean?"

Gran gave Will a meaningful look.

"Dogs and worse."

There was a loud bang.

"That's the fence slamming against the shed," Gran said.

Will peered out of the window. A whole section of fence was swinging back and forth, crashing against the side of the shed.

"Are you going exploring again?" Gran asked.

"I go down to the river every morning," Will said.

"Well, just you be careful."

Will stared. It was the first time either of his grandparents had said anything about safety. Something had changed.

"Your packed lunch is all ready for you," Gran said. "There are some slices of parkin. I know how much you enjoyed it."

"Thanks Gran!"

"Remember your key. We might be out when you get back."

Will was surprised. His grandparents never went out together.

"Where are you going?"

"We're not sure we are, but you never know," Gran said mysteriously.

Will opened the door and felt the wind sting his cheeks. Something had definitely changed. He set off along Owl Heart Lane and turned left. He strode along the winding path that would bring him to the rickety wooden bridge. He came round the final bend and stopped. There was a man on the bridge. He had a toolbox with him.

"You must be Tom and Gertie's grandson," the man said.

Will very nearly laughed. He didn't hear Gran and Granddad's names very often.

"I'm Will. What are you doing?"

"The wind did a bit of damage last night," the man said. "I'm making it safe. I'm George Sutch, by the way."

"Are you Farmer Sutch?"

"I am. I am the latest in a line of Farmer Suthches. My family has worked this land for generations."

"Can I use the bridge?" Will asked.

"Oh no, not until I've made it safe."

Will wondered how he could get to the well. Farmer Sutch seemed to read his mind.

"Don't you worry," he said. "There is another bridge just down there. Follow the path along the stream. You'll come to it in ten minutes or so."

"Thank you," Will said. "Would you like a piece of parkin?"

"Gertie Antrobus's golden syrup parkin," Farmer Sutch said. "I wouldn't turn down a treat like that."

Will handed over the parkin and carried on down the path.

"You're late," Nimbus grumbled when Will finally arrived.

"Sorry," Will said. "Farmer Sutch was working on the rickety bridge. He said it was unsafe."

"Unsafe?"

Nimbus started rubbing his podgy palms together.

"Those were his words? *Unsafe*?"

"Those were his words."

"Oh dear," Nimbus said. "Oh, my giddy goat. Oh, my chilblains. This is bad. This is very bad indeed."

"It's only a few planks that came loose," Will said. "Farmer Sutch will have it repaired today."

"You don't understand," Nimbus said. "This isn't about the bridge. This is about the coming storm. The last time the wind did damage to these parts was twenty years ago."

"I know. You told me. There was a storm."

"It wasn't just one storm," Nimbus said. "It was day after day of fierce storms. The wind was so strong it tore the board clean off the well."

"You mean....?"

"I mean there was nothing stopping all the miscreants and sorcerers, the malevolents and do-badders, the monsters and dark-siders from swarming out of the underworld and into the overworld."

"That sounds bad," Will said.

"This is worse than bad," Nimbus said darkly. "This is a once in a generation disaster. We only just forced the underworld woodland folk back into their dark and filthy lair last time. If they break out this time who knows what will happen."

"Isn't there anything we can do?" Will asked.

"There are all kinds of things we can do," Nimbus said.

"Maybe we can nail down the board," Will said. "That way, the underworld folk will never get out."

Nimbus shook his head.

"That won't work," he said. "You're thinking about the board as if it is just a piece of wood. It is a magic board, Will Antrobus. Magic holds it in place and magic can rip it off."

Nimbus wet his finger and held it up to the wind.

"There's magic in this wind, bad magic, wicked magic, magic to tear the board from the well. No, we'll do our best, but a wind this bad is hard to fight. The underworld folk may well escape. If they do it's up to the likes of us to to stop them doing too much damage before we can force them back inside."

"So we will be able to get them back down the well?"

Nimbus turned his head this way and that, as if weighing up the chances.

"It was touch and go last time and they'll be stronger. Good job we've got a three-seer like you."

"I will do anything you want," Will said.

"I know you will, but one three-seer might not be enough."

"So we go and find another one," Will said.

"It's not that easy," Nimbus said. "They don't come along that often."

"There must have been one last time," Will said. "You got the underworld folk back in the well so you must have had a three-seer to help you."

"I did," Nimbus said.

"Can't we ask this person to help?"

Nimbus shook his head.

"It won't work," he said. "She's grown up now. Three-seers turn into one-seers, two-seers at best when they grow up. The day they turn thirteen that's it. They might as well have never had the sight at all."

"But who is she? We've got to try."

"Don't you know?" Nimbus said.

Will was puzzled.

"No."

"The last storm was twenty years ago," Nimbus said. "There was a special child in Greengate at that time, an eleven-year-old girl called Holly."

Will couldn't believe his ears.

"Holly! You mean my mum is a three-seer."

"She was one of the greatest of all three-seers. She could see things the way they seemed to be. She could see the way they really were under the skin. But on a good day, if she tried really heard, why, she could see right into the very heart of things. The day she grew up we lost a great champion."

Will was quiet for a few moments before he found his voice.

"There's only one thing for it," he said. "I'm going to get her back."

Chapter Nineteen
"Try to remember."

Will was starting to see what Nimbus meant by patterns. He went back over the photographs on his grandparents' walls. Whether they were colour photographs or black and white ones, whether they were line drawings or watercolours, somewhere in the background, in the shadows, if you looked very carefully, there was a hidden, twisted, wicked-looking face. That wasn't all. In the foreground, so obvious he wondered why he had never noticed it before, there was a child about his age, somewhere between eight and twelve, but never any older than that.

Some of the pictures were dated. Will scampered off to his room and came back with a notepad and a pencil. He started with the

most recent, the one of his mum twenty years earlier then he went step by step back in time. He read the list of dates and his discovery leapt out at him. Every twenty years, give or take a year, there was a great storm. Every twenty years there was an underworld woodland spirit in the shadows. Even more exciting, every twenty years there was a child about his age. In one of them, from forty years ago, there were two children, a boy and a girl.

"Who are they, Gran?" Will asked.

"Why, that's your Granddad and that's me."

"You knew each other when you were kids?"

"Of course we did. I grew up in this very cottage and your Granddad lived just down the lane at Boar Lodge."

"He lived in one of the lodges?" Will asked. "The ones with the animal carvings on the wall."

"He did indeed. We went to the same school and when we grew up we started courting. It seemed the natural thing to do."

"That's so cool!" Will said.

He had an idea.

"Look closely at those trees, Gran," he said. "Do you see anything?"

Gran tipped her glasses forward on her nose.

"I can see shadows. What are you getting at, Will?"

"Try looking into the shadows. Look really hard. Don't you see it?"

Gran shook her head.

"All I can see is shadows. Why, what do you think you can see?"

"There's a face," Will said. "There are faces in all these pictures."

Gran stared, as if she was haunted by a memory, then she burst out laughing.

"You and your imagination, Will Antrobus. Anyway, I can't be hanging round here chatting to you. I've got to go down to the village shop for a few things."

She glanced at the clock on the wall.

"Holly will be down before long."

Will was disappointed. He was sure that Mum and Gran and Granddad were three-seers just like him. When they were children they had discovered Nimbus sitting by his well. He had granted them wishes. All those other children, maybe they were his Great-Granddad and Grandma, his Great-Great Granddad and Grandma and so it went on. But why did they lose the ability to see things the way they were as soon as they started to grow up? He had some questions for Nimbus.

"I think I'll go out to play," he said.

"Your Granddad is still mending the fence," Gran said. "He might pop out for nails or something so take your key with you."

"When is Mum coming?"

"She'll be here by tea-time. She is going to stay for a day or two." She lowered her voice. "I think she's had a bit of a falling out with your Dad."

Will thought it was odd that two of the three people who lived in his house were going to be staying with his grandparents, but he didn't really understand grow-ups. The rickety wooden bridge was mended so it wasn't quite as rickety as it had been. He raced through the roaring wind to the water meadow and scrambled inside the thicket. Nimbus was waiting for him.

"How old are you?" Will said.

"Why do you ask?"

"Well, you knew my Mum when she was a little girl. I think you knew my grandparents too. Did you?"

"Yes, I knew Tom and Gertie when they were children."

"They were three-seers too, weren't they?"

"They were," Nimbus said. "You're learning, Will Antrobus."

"Have all my family been three-seers?"

"Yes. Your Gran and Granddad are special. It is the only time I know of when there were two three-seers growing up in the village at the same time."

"So," Will said, remembering his original question, "how old are you?"

"In human years?"

"Is there any other way of counting?" Will said.

"There are many other ways," Nimbus said. "Sprites count in hours because they don't live very long. Gnomes like me count in seasons. Goblins count in storm years. Witches and warlocks count in centuries."

"So how old *are* you?" Will asked, getting frustrated. Why did Nimbus always take so long to get to the point?

"I'm four hundred seasons young," Nimbus said.

"So you're a hundred years old!"

"That's about right."

"So you must have seen five great storms."

"I have."

"And the underworld folk have escaped five times in your life?"

"Oh no," Nimbus said. "Only three times."

Will didn't understand.

"The underworld folk have been getting stronger. The first two times we were able to stop them getting out. When Tom and Gertie were young a couple of goblins got loose, but we soon caught them."

"What about when Mum was a little girl?"

"Oh, that was a real battle, that was. There were goblins and sprites, witches and warlocks all over the county. We had a devil of a time rounding them up."

"But you got them eventually?"

"Yes."

"Mum went missing for a while, didn't she?"

"Oh, you know about that, do you?"

"Yes, Granddad said."

Nimbus nodded, as if remembering something.

"She was gone all night. She never said where she had been, but it made her stronger. She learned the deepest magic. Just when it looked like the underworld folk would take over the county, Holly turned the tide of battle."

"So I need to find out where she went?"

"Sooner or later the underworld folk will break free and wreak havoc on the county. If we can discover the secret of where Holly went and how it made her strong, we might just overcome the mischief-makers."

"But that means a three-seer can make a wish after dark. You said that was impossible."

"I said it wasn't a good idea. A wish is pretty safe in daylight hours. After dark it can get out of hand."

"Mum used hers after dark. She must have done if she went missing all night."

"She did," Nimbus said. "To this day it's a complete mystery where she went."

"What did she wish for that night?"

Nimbus hesitated.

"Nimbus?"

"I gave her an open wish. She said she didn't know what she was going to wish for, but she would know when she found it."

"She's coming home at tea time," Will said. "I'm going to ask her about the wish."

He realised what he had said. London wasn't home any more. Greengate was.

The Second Story

Underworld

Chapter One
Mum's home

"Mum!"

Will raced down the path and gave her a huge hug.

"That's a nice welcome," Mum said. "Are you feeling homesick?"

The smile drained from his face.

"You've not come to take me home, have you?"

"It sounds like you're having a good time in sleepy old Greengate," Mum said.

"It's not that sleepy at the moment," Will said, hoping she would get the hint and begin to remember.

"The wind, you mean?" Mum said. "It is a bit wild. The weather wasn't this bad in London. It's been getting worse all the way up."

"Why do you think that is?" Will asked eagerly, still hoping the gathering storm would jog her memory.

Mum just tapped the end of his nose with her finger.

"Maybe it's because my mischief of a son is whipping up trouble."

With that, she went over to talk to Gran and Granddad. Will was disappointed. Was there nothing left of the little girl who had once discovered Nimbus sitting on his well? Was there nothing left of the three-seer she had been?

"I've just repaired that fence," Granddad was saying. "It's going

93

to be a bad storm, make no mistake. We haven't seen anything like this for twenty years. I bet you've forgotten the great storm."

"How could I forget?" Mum said. "Do you remember when Mrs Haddock's chimney stack came crashing down?"

Gran and Granddad nodded.

"I went missing, didn't I?"

"You did," Granddad said. "I searched for you high and low."

"I wonder where I went," Mum said. "Isn't it strange that I don't remember."

She thought of something.

"I lost my lucky charm bracelet."

"Anyway," Gran said, "I've got a nice cottage pie in the oven. Are you hungry?"

"Starving," Mum said. "I've only had a sandwich and a bag of crisps on the way up."

"That won't satisfy your appetite," Gran said. "There's nothing like home made food, is there Will?"

Will shook his head. He still felt disappointed. He had really been hoping that the storm would bring memories of the past back, but nothing seemed to remind them of the woodland folk and the underworld invasion. Over the dinner table they talked about the weather and things that had been happening in the wider world. Nobody returned to subject of the great storm of twenty years before.

Eventually, Will went up to bed and sat reading a book about the history of Greengate he had found on the shelf on the landing. He had always dreamed of finding a book of spells. He discovered a chapter about the lodges. It explained how the lodges were spaced out in a circle around the village, seven of them in all. Each one showed a different animal. Some of them were real. Some were from ancient myths and legends. He read the names:

"Monkey lodge, boar lodge, eagle lodge, wolf lodge, deer lodge, gryphon lodge...."

"Dragon lodge," came a voice.

Will glanced at the door. Mum was standing there, smiling.

"I haven't heard anyone talk about the lodges since I was a little girl," she said. "What are you reading?"

Will showed her the book. Mum perched on the edge of the bed. "I loved this little book when I was a child!" she exclaimed. "Fancy you choosing the very same book I took off the shelf when I was your age. Just look at those photographs. The animals are so real. You can imagine them leaping out of the wall and...."

She frowned. Suddenly, Will was excited.

"What, Mum? They could leap out of the wall and what?"

She stared down at the page for a few moments.

"I don't know. I don't know what I was going to say."

"You do, Mum. I know you do. You were going to say that they could leap out of the wall and run and scamper and fly around Greengate. That's it, isn't it?"

She looked at him for a moment then grinned and tousled his hair.

"You've got a vivid imagination, Will."

"It's not imagination, Mum," he protested. "Just try to remember. Cast your mind back to the night of the great storm. You went out to play. You must remember."

"I went out to play every single morning that summer," Mum said. "Whatever are you getting at?"

"I know where you went," Will said. "Every day you set off along Owl Heart Lane and turned left. You followed a winding path to a rickety wooden bridge. You went along a rough track around the edge of Farmer Sutch's field. From there you went along the river and through a water meadow. On the far side of the meadow there was a thicket."

"Oh, you've been playing near my childhood haunts, have you?"

"Please try to remember, Mum. You crept inside the thicket and there he was."

"There who was?"

"Nimbus! Nimbus the gnome!"

This time there was no long look, no frown and no suspicion that she might, just for a moment, be remembering strange events from her childhood. Instead, Mum burst out laughing.

"Oh Will, you really are the limit! So you've got an invisible friend called Nimbus the gnome."

"He isn't invisible," Will cried. "He is...visible. I've seen him. *You've* seen him!"

Mum gave him a kiss on the forehead.

"Night, night, Will. Sleep tight. If you need something to help you doze off, don't count sheep. Try gnomes instead."

Chapter Two
Nobody believes me

"You don't seem yourself this morning," Nimbus said as Will wormed his way inside the thicket.

"Mum thinks I'm making it all up," Will said. "She says I've got an overactive imagination. I asked if she remembered you, but she didn't."

Nimbus looked troubled.

"You mentioned my name?"

"Yes, of course."

"But not to anyone else, I hope."

"I wouldn't do that!" Will cried. "I thought Mum would remember. She's a three-seer."

"Something happens when you humans grow up," Nimbus said. "They lose the clear sightedness of childhood. When you are children you believe in magic and other worlds. You think pigs can fly and dogs can talk. You think you can grow wings in the night…"

"Or grow fins and swim down the river?"

"Exactly. You think anything is possible. Then something happens. You stop believing."

"But why?" Will asked. "Why does it have to happen?"

"I'm a gnome," Nimbus said. "I live in a world where anything is possible, good or bad. Don't ask me to live in the world of men and women."

"Well, it isn't fair," Will said. "We need her help."

"We won't get it," Nimbus said. "When the storm finally breaks this evening, it will be down to you and I and anyone Cirrus can muster."

"Am I going to meet him?" Will asked excitedly.

"You are indeed," Nimbus said. "You will meet Cirrus and a large number of other gnomes. We will try to hold the board in place, but if the storm is very bad we are in for a wild night. The mischief-makers are bound to break free."

"Will it be very bad?" Will asked.

"We only just got them back last time," Nimbus said. "This time they will be stronger."

Will looked at the racing, violet clouds and felt the bite of the wind on his face. Somewhere in the distance thunder was rumbling.

"I wish I had super-strength to hold down the board," he said.

"Be careful what you wish for?" Nimbus said. "I can grant you

strength, but I can't be sure it will be enough to keep the lid on. Wishes are not all powerful. They are one kind of magic against another. The three-seer has to make the right choice."

"So you think super-strength is the wrong choice?" Will asked.

"I can't tell you what to choose," Nimbus said. "That is up to you."

Will took the hint.

"I will choose something different, but what? Did Mum always make the right choices?"

Nimbus laughed.

"Are you joking? When she first came to visit me she chose to bring her doll to life and that was in the middle of an imp breakout."

"So it wasn't very good?"

"It was very bad. The doll turned out to be very naughty and started helping the imps. That wasn't meant to happen."

"I see."

"It took Holly some time to learn. You take after her."

Will liked that.

"Do I?'

"Oh yes."

"So how did he get the mischief-makers back in the well?" Will asked. "You haven't told me that."

"She wished for a giant net carried by a dragon, a gryphon and an eagle."

"How did she come up with a wish like that?" Will wondered out loud. "I mean, it isn't the kind of thing you think of every day."

"That I don't know. She vanished for hours then, just as the battle seemed to be lost, she appeared riding on the eagle's back with the dragon and gryphon either side of her, the net dangling between them."

"She brought the creatures from the lodges to life!"

"You're right. The question is- how did she do it?"

"She never told me," Nimbus said sadly. "That last great battle took place at the end of the summer. It was time for her to go back to school. I didn't see much of her after that. She was entering the time of not believing."

"I've got to find out where she went," Will said.

Nimbus scratched his chin under his beard.

"How are you going to do that, Will Antrobus?"

"I don't know," Will said, "but I have to find a way. I'll be back."

"Get back before the light dies," Nimbus said. "That's when the mischief-makers will try to break out."

"I know."

"Once the sun goes down, the night becomes dangerous and so do wishes. Grant a wish in daylight and you have a good idea where it is going to end. Grant one at night, well, there's no saying how it will turn out."

Will was no longer listening. He sprinted away towards Farmer Sutch's field.

He would get Mum to remember. He had to.

Chapter Three
One heck of a wind

He was in for a disappointment when he got back to his grandparents' cottage. Mum was nowhere to be found.

"Where did she go?" Will asked.

"I don't know," Granddad said. "She was talking about when she was a little girl."

Will's heart kicked.

"What did she say?"

"Only that she would like to visit some of the haunts of her childhood."

For Will, that only meant one place.

"You mean she went down by the river?'

"No," Granddad said, "I don't think so. I watched her go and she turned right rather than left at the end of Owl Heart Lane.

"So she went into the village?"

"Possibly," Granddad said. "Mind you, the house where I grew up is down that way. She used to love me telling her about my adventures when I was a little boy."

Will thought of something.

"You grew up in Boar Lodge, didn't you?"

"That's right. It stayed in the family until my old mum died, then we sold it to a family moving into the area."

"I'm going to find her," Will said.

He raced down Owl Heart Lane and turned right. He expected

to find Mum standing looking at Boar Lodge. Maybe the sight of the carved stone boar would bring back the past. To his surprise, she wasn't there. After what Granddad had said, Will was sure she would be. He hurried through into the village, peering down alleys. Where was she? Where could she have gone? He stopped by the stone cross in the square. For a few moments he looked right and left along the High Street. She was nowhere to be seen. Then he happened to glance at the stone cross itself and was amazed by what he saw. There was a circle carved into the base and at regular points on the circle there was a carving.

"The animals!" Will exclaimed.

"That's right," said the elderly gentleman who was sitting on a bench opposite with his wife. "The carving represents the seven animals that protect the village. If you carry on up the hill you will come to the next one. When I was your age I used to go on a walk to see all seven."

That's what Mum is doing, Will thought. It makes sense.

"Thank you," Will said and set off along the route Mum must have taken.

He found Monkey Lodge at the top of the hill. Maybe half a mile out of town he came across Deer Lodge, but there was still no sign of Mum. After that, he found the first six of the lodges, but no Mum. He was starting to lose hope when he turned a corner and there she was, leaning on a gate. There was a For Sale sign in the garden.

"Mum?"

"Will! How did you know where to find me?"

"I saw what was on the stone cross in the village and worked it out."

She looked surprised.

"You're a very bright boy, you know that?"

"You're starting to remember, aren't you?" he said. "You know

something happened the night of the great storm."

"You're right," she said, gazing at the tossing oaks along the lane. "I've been thinking about those times a lot. Last night I had the strangest dream. It must be you going on about your friend, the gnome."

Will was overjoyed.

"So you remember Nimbus?"

But Mum brought him down with a bump.

"Will, I thought we'd been through this," she said. "Gnomes aren't real."

"But they are! Nimbus is as real as you or I."

"Now Will, don't go making things up again."

"I'm not making it up. Why won't you listen to me?"

He saw the look on her face. This wasn't getting him anywhere. He remembered what she said about her dreams.

"What did you dream?"

"No, it's silly."

"Please tell me, Mum," he begged.

"Oh, all right, if you must know I dreamed I was riding on the back of a giant bird." She pointed at the eagle "It was this very one here. In my dream it tore itself off the wall and soared into the sky."

"What happened after that?"

"I really don't remember," Mum said. "I know I was very, very frightened, but there was something more important than fear, something that made me urge the eagle onward into the darkness."

"What was it?"

"I don't know," Mum said. "I woke up before the dream ended."

"It's real," Will said. "That dream of yours is real. Twenty years ago the eagle broke free from the wall." He pointed to the stone eagle. "This wall. So did all the other stone animals. Somehow you made them help you against the mischief-makers."

Mum stared at him wide-eyed.

"I knew you had a big imagination," she said, "but that is one heck of a story."

"And this is one heck of a wind," Will said. "Don't you know what's going to happen tonight? All kinds of goblins and imps, witches and warlocks are going to break out from the underworld and cause all kinds of mischief."

The words came tumbling out in a rush. He was quite out of breath.

"You do remember, don't you?" he cried. "You've got to."

He willed her to say she did, but her answer was like a slap in the face.

"No Will, I don't remember any such thing. Let's get you home. I think Granddad's been filling your head with all kinds of silly nonsense. Stone animals don't come to life. They never have and they never will."

Chapter Four
Another great storm

Gran saw Will putting his coat on.

"Where do you think you're going, young man?"

"I'm going out exploring."

"Your tea is going to be ready in an hour or two," Gran said. "Besides, you never go out this late."

She glanced out of the window.

"The weather is awful. Just listen to that wind. No, you can't go out in this weather."

"But I've got to!"

"Not when there is a storm brewing you don't," Gran said. "Now put your coat back on the peg and find something else to do."

"But...."

Gran did her best to put on her stern face.

"No more buts, Will Antrobus. Hang your coat up and find yourself something to do around the house."

Will started to protest again, but Gran wasn't having any of it.

"Now that's enough!" she said, as close to angry as he had ever seen her.

Will trudged upstairs and sat on the edge of his bed. What was he going to do? Nimbus would be waiting for him. So would all the other gnomes. He sat down with his book, the one with the pictures of the stone animals, but he was too miserable to read. That's when he glimpsed movement out of the corner of his eye.

It was the owl that had visited him the day he arrived

"I know what you want," Will said. "You want me to go and see Nimbus. I can't. Gran won't let me."

The owl blinked then flew in a circle, hovering a little way away.

"What are you doing?" Will asked.

The owl did it again, flying in a tight, little loop then hovering in the same place. Will went to the window and understood immediately. Just under the window was a sturdy branch. If it could take his wait he could crawl along it and climb down into the garden. That way nobody would see him leave the cottage. He struggled for a moment to get the window open. The wind kept pushing it back. Finally, he shoved it open, squeezed through and shut it behind him. The branch creaked a little, but he was able to make his way along it and clamber down to the ground. He had never done anything like this before. He had always tried to be good, but he didn't see any other way. He was on his way out of the drive when somebody spotted him. He heard a shout, but he wasn't going to stop for anyone. He started to run.

"Will!"

It was Mum.

At the end of the lane he turned left.

"Will!"

He didn't stop. He ran and ran, over the rickety bridge, around Farmer Sutch's field, across the water meadow and along the river to the thicket.

"Is something wrong?" Nimbus said the moment he saw Will's face.

"I ran away," Will said, not feeling at all good about what he had done.

"It was bound to happen," Nimbus said. "A three-seer sees things an adult can't. It always causes problems."

"Did Mum run away from Gran and Granddad?" Will asked.

"Oh yes," Nimbus told him. "She was always doing it. She was much more of a problem than you, though she was slightly older, almost a teenager."

Will thought about all the times Mum had told him to pay attention to what she was saying. Did she say one thing and do another? He was starting to see her in a new light.

"Will," Nimbus said, "haven't you noticed anything?"

"No," Will said.

"Really?"

Will looked around and his eyes widened like full moons. On every branch and every stone, all around the well and on top of the board there were gnomes and not just gnomes like Nimbus with fluffy white beards. There were female gnomes too, though they didn't have beards at all. There were even little boy and girl gnomes.

"So what do you say to Will?" Nimbus said.

"Hello Will," the gnomes chorused.

"We'd better get to work," Nimbus said.

Many of the gnomes were carrying a ball of thread. It wasn't really string. It was finer than string and it came in all kinds of

colours. There was scarlet and emerald, sapphire and violet, silver and gold.

"What are you going to do?" Will asked.

"We are going to bind the well."

"I thought you couldn't just tie it down," Will said, remembering an earlier conversation. "Isn't it all about magic."

"This is magic," Nimbus said. "These are magic threads made from flutterfly silk."

"Don't you mean butterfly?" Will said.

"I mean flutterfly," Nimbus said. "Flutterflies are rarer than butterflies. Only the woodland folk can see them...and three-seers of course."

"Do you think it will work?" Will asked.

Nimbus rolled up his sleeves.

"There is only one way to find out."

Chapter Five
Mum

Soon the thicket was a hive of activity. Some of the gnomes raced round and round the well, encircling it with multi-coloured thread. Others threw weighted threads over the board until hundreds of threads criss crossed the well and the board. It wasn't long before the well was completely encased in a cocoon of many colours.

"It doesn't even look like a well," Will said.

"What does it look like?" Nimbus said.

"I don't know, a kind of cap made out of a rainbow."

Nimbus laughed.

"That's a very good description."

At that very moment the rainbow cap jumped.

"Oh oh," one of the gnomes said.

"It's starting," another added.

"The wind is getting under the thread," Will said.

Sure enough the gale was now howling through the thicket and whipping round well. The board was banging and thumping.

"Everybody grab the end of a thread!" Nimbus shouted.

Within moments every dwarf was tugging at a thread, struggling to hold the board in place. As the board rattled and banged, jumped and thumped, many of the gnomes were tumbling or skidding across the ground.

"Dig your heels in," Nimbus ordered. "We've got to hold it."

Now it wasn't just the sound of the wind. From inside the well came cackling and chuckling, yelling and shouting, squabbling and snarling.

"It's them," Nimbus cried. "The mischief makers are trying to break out."

The gnomes redoubled their efforts, heaving with all their might. Soon their faces were bright red with the effort.

"Climb on top of the board!" Nimbus roared.

Will sprang onto the board. It was difficult to stand. It was bouncing up and down and swaying from side to side. He could hear the voices of the mischief-makers bubbling up from inside the well. He could even hear Pricklepot's familiar voice.

"You thought you'd got rid of me, didn't you boy? Well, think again. I'm going to have so much fun when I get out."

"Hold them!" Nimbus shouted. "Pull. Pull with all your might!"

But no matter how hard the gnomes pulled, no matter how they tugged and heaved, the board was jumping and leaping ever more wildly. Just as Will was struggling to keep his balance, the branches of the thicket parted and there was Mum.

"Will," she said. "You were told to stay in the house. How could you....?"

She didn't finish the sentence. She had seen the gnomes pulling on the coloured threads and the board leaping and jumping. She had heard the noises coming from the well.

"No," she said. "No, it can't be."

"It's happening, Mum," Will yelled, struggling to keep his footing. "You can see what is happening with your own eyes."

"No," Mum repeated. "I refuse to believe it."

With that, she turned and fled.

"Mum!" Will cried.

He wanted to go after her, but he couldn't leave the board. If he climbed down, the mischief-makers would surely escape.

"Don't go after her," Nimbus pleaded. "We need your help."

"I'm staying," Will said.

Even with his help, it was far from certain that they could hold the board down. The pressure from below was getting stronger and stronger. The roar of the wind was getting more powerful. Trying to stand on the board was like riding a tidal wave.

"I'm going to fall!" Will warned.

"You've got to stay on," Nimbus told him.

Then there was a new problem. Ping, ping, ping went some of the threads.

"They're snapping," groaned some of the gnomes.

It was true. One by one at first, then in groups, the many coloured threads were snapping. Soon it was like the crackle of popcorn. As the sound became deafening, the board tore loose and started to spin wildly round the thicket. Will couldn't hold on any longer and went flying into the air before crashing to the ground in a heap.

"Ow!"

He looked up in panic and saw the board spinning away like a frisbee.

"That does it," Nimbus said.

Already imps and sprites were swarming out of the well. There were green-faced goblins and black-caped witches, wicked-looking warlocks and all sorts of brownies and gremlins and elves. Pricklepot stopped for a moment to gloat in front of Will. "I told you it wasn't over," he sneered. "It's show time!"

The gnomes were the first victims of the mischief-makers. The imps and sprites tugged their beards. The witches seized them by their braces and carried them off towards the river.

"Time for a swim," they cackled.

The hobgoblins plucked the remaining gnomes off the ground and left them dangling in trees, but the gnomes weren't the mischief-makers' main targets.

"Those rascally humans have had their own way too long," said Pricklepot. "What do you say, Hob?"

Hob was the biggest, greenest, ugliest goblin of them all. Will guessed he was their king. Hob gave a hideous laugh.

"Let the wild mayhem begin!"

Chapter Six
Mayhem....

Nearby Kingsford was the first town to feel the wrath of the mischief-makers. The Mayor, Elisabeth Flump, was addressing the council's annual dinner in the Town Hall.

"So, ladies and gentlemen," she said, "we continue to serve the people of Kingsford to the best of our ability."

The councillors clapped loudly.

"So let us eat a hearty dinner and congratulate ourselves on another successful year."

Little did she know that one of the witch queens, Griselda Grizzle was watching from a window.

"A hearty dinner, is it?" she chuckled.

She watched the scene for a few moments than started to weave a spell.

"Before these piglets can stuff their faces,

let's put their food through its paces.

Spoons are ready to start the soup,

Now watch it do the loop de loop."

Instantly the potato and leek soup started to quiver.

"Whatever is happening?" Mayor Flump wondered out loud.

A moment later she found out. The soup leapt out of its bowl, spun round and round her startled head, then slapped itself - slop - all over her gown.

"Oh."

Some people gasped. Others laughed. It made no difference what they did. They too watched in horror as their own bowl of soup took to the air before depositing itself over their chests.

"What do you make of that?" asked Councillor Arnold Snivel.

After some discussion, the diners decided that it was a freak accident caused by the draughts in the hall.

"It's this storm," Mayor Flump said. "I haven't seen anything like it in twenty years."

Satisfied with her first attempt, Griselda Grizzle, waited for the main course to arrive before weaving her second spell.

"The guests are looking forward to their roast chicken.
Let loose the magic, start the flicking."

As forks hovered over gravy-drenched chicken breasts, the meat suddenly leapt from the plate. The slower diners were immediately showered in food. The lucky ones ducked, but their ordeal wasn't over.

"Make the jelly very smelly,
make the custard taste like mustard."

Soon guests were pulling faces. One ran to the toilet to be sick.

114

Griselda was only just getting into her stride.

"Let the ice cream really scream,
watch the pudding let off steam,
round and round the table go,
make blancmange fall like snow."

By now the unfortunate councillors were fleeing through a hail of food. It pattered in their hair. It splattered on their cheeks. There was no escape from the flying food.

"I'm getting out of here," Arnold Snivel announced.

"Me too," Grizelda Grizzle said.

But they were going nowhere.

"While the food falls with a splat,
make their tyres go completely flat."

The councillors stared in disbelief. Not one vehicle in the car park was in any state to move. Little did they know that Grizelda was already working on her next spell.

"You can walk away if you really try,
But please watch out,
A pie can.....fly!"

Sure enough, apple and cherry pies were soon soaring through the darkness, scattering the guests. Still, the councillors' torment wasn't over. Sprites were waiting in the bushes. They pinched bottoms and tugged hair. They rolled marbles under running feet. In short, they did everything they could to make their victims squeal with fright.

Soon imp and sprite, brownie and elf alike were stuffing themselves with what was left of the banquet. They chomped and scoffed, munched and crunched, swallowed and burped until there was nothing left, not a morsel, nothing at all. That's when Grizelda spotted the portraits of mayor and councillors, past and present. Before you could say the word doodle, her fellow mischief-makers were scribbling away at the portraits.

They drew horns and glasses and fangs. They added donkey's ears and monkey's tails. They drew beards on the faces of the women and lipstick on the mouths of the men.

"You just wait until they look at themselves up there tomorrow," Grizelda chuckled.

The mischief-makers declared their night at the Town Hall a great success.

"They won't forget the night of their dinner in a hurry," she said. Then she hopped on her broomstick and zigzagged away across the sky.

"Look lively," she said. "There's mischief to be made."

Chapter Seven
....and more mayhem

Over in Puddington the town's talent contest was getting underway. Fans were queuing round the block to see what the three judges had to say about the local hopefuls. They walked on stage to deafening cheers. Master of ceremonies Jim Miniman announced them one by one.

"Ladies and gentlemen," he said, "welcome the judges. First up, lead singer of Tune-Free Zone, Kelly McGorgeous."

There was loud applause.

"Now meet the man who always says what he thinks. Yes, it's Gordon Grumbleguts."

There was more applause and a few boos.

"And finally, the handsomest man the whole county, Marvin Mirrorhugger."

The judges took their seats and waited for the first act to begin. Little did they know that this was going to be a contest like no other. Up in the gantry overlooking the stage Hob and his goblins were watching with interest. Jim Miniman introduced the first act.

"Starting tonight's show- it's our favourite pop band Tone Deaf."

Hob listened to the three singers then glanced left and right at his fellow goblins.

"Tone Deaf by name and tone deaf by nature," he grumbled.

Tone Deaf started their dance routine and raised their

microphones to their mouths for the second score.

"It's more than a goblin can take," Hob chuckled with a sly wink. He swooped behind the band and reached in his pocket for a small packet of what looked like dust.

"Make this night really rich,
watch these singers start to itch."

He opened the packet and blew it over the singers. The effect was instant and dramatic. First one, then two, then all three members of Tone Deaf started to twitch and twist, wriggle and writhe, rub and scratch. The judges swapped startled glances. Within moments the Tone Deaf boys were rolling round on the stage howling like dogs as they tore at their skin. Finally Jim Miniman appeared.

"Well judges," he said. "What's your opinion of...er...that?"

He looked at Kelly McGorgeous.

"I thought it was a very interesting take on a classic song," she said. "It really spoke to me."

The crowd whooped and cheered.

It was Gordon Grumbleguts' turn.

"Gordon?"

"Are you kidding, Kelly?" Gordon sneered. "They were awful. My dog can sing better. As for the dancing, it sucked. In fact it was the suckingest dancing I have ever had the misfortune to watch."

The crowd booed.

"Right to the point as usual," Jim said. "What about you, Marvin?"

"I *loved* it," Marvin cooed. "When I was singing with Beyonce in Vegas. I know Beyonce, of course. When I was singing with Beyonce in Vegas I performed the song just like that and the crowd went wild. Let's go to the vote."

Jim nodded.

"Kelly?"

"It's a yes from me."

"Gordon."

"A definite no. They stunk the house out."

The crowd booed.

"You have got the deciding vote, Marvin."

"It's a...."

The crowd leaned forward in their seats.

"....yes!"

The crowd went wild. Gordon got out of his seat and started to storm out of the arena red-faced. That's when Hob decided to play his second trick.

"This Gordon guy is far too lippy,

let's make the floor kind of slippy."

Sure enough, Gordon skidded and flipped high in the air, landing with a bump on his bottom. The crowd howled with laughter. Gordon scrambled to his feet and fell again. The crowd roared.

"Somebody help me," Gordon growled.

Kelly tottered over on her high heels and she too went sprawling, collapsing in a pile with all the grace of a baby giraffe on ice. Soon

Jim and Marvin were sent tumbling as they tried to help. Once the people in the audience had stopped laughing they started to ask each other what on earth was happening. Already, Hob was working on his next practical joke.

"Now forget about the slippy floors

Lets see what happens when it rains indoors."

The words were barely out of his twisted, green mouth when driving rain started to hammer down on the unfortunate spectators. They squealed and did their best to cover their heads. Soon, the already treacherous floor was swimming with water. As the spectators tried to leave the hall they were carried down the streaming aisles to the stage where they lay flapping like beached whales.

Chapter Eight
Going underground

"You've got to grant me a wish," Will said as he watched the mischief-makers vanish in all directions.

"You haven't told me the wish," Nimbus said.

"That's because I don't know what it is yet."

Nimbus looked puzzled.

"So how can I grant it?"

"Can't you grant it in advance so it comes true when I know what it is I want?" Will asked.

"You want an open wish?" Nimbus said.

"Yes."

"You want me to trust you to choose sensibly?"

"Yes."

"You want....?"

"Yes, yes, yes!" Will cried, losing patience. "We don't have much time, Nimbus. Can you imagine the things those creatures are getting up to?"

"Unfortunately," Nimbus answered, "I can."

"So just do it. Please."

Nimbus sighed and did as Will said.

"But how will you know what to wish for?" he asked.

"Simple," Will said. "I'm going down there."

He pointed down the well.

"You can't!"

"Why not?"

"Oh, it's a wicked place, that is."

"Have you been?"

"No, never. No gnome has set foot down there in many a long year. We left the underworld many years ago to make our peace with humankind. We have no wish to go back." A shadow crossed his face. "My old dad went down there to try to make peace between the mischief-makers and the humans. He never came back."

"Well, I'm going," Will said stubbornly.

"Why?" Nimbus asked.

"Simple," Will said. "I think that's where Mum was the night she went missing. Granddad said he looked everywhere. The well is the obvious place."

"Nimbus peered into the gloom."

"You could be right, but I don't think you should go."

"Are you going to stop me? Will said.

Nimbus shook his head.

"It's your choice, Will Antrobus."

Without another word, Will straddled the well and looked for the best way down.

"It's very dark."

Nimbus reached into the undergrowth and pulled out a lantern. He snapped his fingers and a yellowish light bathed the thicket. Will took it and saw the footholds he was going to use to make his descent.

"Good luck, Will," Nimbus said.

"Thanks."

The walls were slippery and the footholds few, but soon Will was halfway down. He glanced up and saw Nimbus' head silhouetted against the moonlight. Will continued on his way. Before he got as far as the dark, stagnant water he saw a tunnel branch off to his left. He reached across and made his way inside. The lantern illuminated the walls. Tree roots poked through the walls. He couldn't stand up in the narrow tunnel. He had to crawl. Presently he came to a large chamber and he was able to stand up. He looked around. There wasn't much to see really, it was just an empty space from which several passages branched. "Which way do I go?" Will wondered out loud.

That's when he glimpsed something shining in the glow of the lantern. Will bent down and reached for the sparkling object.

"It's a charm bracelet," he said.

He rubbed off the dirt. There was a name engraved on one of the charms. Holly.

"It's Mum's bracelet," he said, "the one she lost."

The bracelet lay by the mouth of the third of the branches.

"This must be it. I was right. Mum did come down here that night."

He put the bracelet in his pocket and crawled along the tunnel on his hands and knees.

"I wonder what I'll find," he said out loud.

To his surprise, he got an answer from the other end of the tunnel.

"Keep going and you will have your answer."

"Who are you?" Will asked, hesitating.

"Just keep coming."

Will followed the tunnel and presently it opened up into a second chamber. To his surprise there was a small and very old gnome squatting opposite him.

"You're a gnome."

"I'm the gnome who was foolish enough to come down here to make peace," the gnome said.

Will saw the reason why he never got out again. The gnome's leg was shackled and chained.

"Who did this to you?" Will asked.

"They did."

"The mischief-makers?"

"That's right. I held them off while my brothers and sisters escaped. This is the price I paid for blocking the mischief-makers' way."

"How long have you been here?"

"Years and years and years."

"Poor you!"

"That's what the little girl said," the gnome grunted. "She said she would return to set me free, but she never did. She forgot all about me the way children do when they grow up into...." He spat the next word out, "....teenagers."

"That little girl was my mum," Will said.

"You're Holly's son?"

"That's right."

"Is it that long?" the gnome groaned sadly. "I wish I could get

out of these chains and see the world above just once."

Will edged closer.

"Tell me what Mum discovered down here and I will make sure you do."

"You'll only forget."

"I won't," Will said. "I promise."

The gnome glanced at him.

"It doesn't matter whether you remember or not," the elderly gnome said. "I'll tell you anyway."

"Thank you," Will said. "What's your name?"

"I'm Pileus."

"That wouldn't be a cloud, would it?"

"Yes."

"Do you know somebody called Nimbus?"

A tear spilled down Pileus' cheek.

"He's my little boy."

"Your son?"

"Yes."

"I know him," Will said.

"You can take me to my son?"

"Yes, just tell me what you know."

Pileus started to tell his tale.

Chapter Nine
"I remember!"

At about this time the crazy imp Pricklepot reached Greengate.
He was determined to do as much damage as he could and he
started with the things that gave him his name.
"Get yourself a club each, boys," he shouted.
"A what?" Windnoggin asked.
"A stick used to play golf, idiot."
The imps scampered off and returned with sticks that resembled
golf clubs. Windnoggin was holding a twig about the size of a
pencil.
"Give me strength!" Pricklepot groaned. "Are you a complete
idiot?"
"I think I may be," said Windnoggin.
Pricklepot just shook his head.
"It's smashing time," he cried.
Soon there was an imp on every roof in the village, getting ready
to swing with all his might.
"Now!" Pricklepot shouted with all his might.
The imps swung. The chimney pots smashed. Within moments
the householders came rushing outside. That only made things
worse. The imps started to pelt them with roof tiles. The
householders fled back indoors.
"Got one!" Windnoggin shouted.
All the imps turned to look and started cackling with laughter.

"That's not a club, Windnoggin," Pricklepot said. "It's a dog lead."

In the Antrobus family cottage, Granddad was brushing fragments of roof tile from his clothes.

"It's happening again," he said. "There's another great wind, just like the one twenty years ago."

Mum had just got back from looking for Will. She had already forgotten what she had seen.

"Are you sure it's just the wind?" she said, a doubt creeping into her mind. "I thought I heard a voice."

"A voice?" Gran said. "You're imagining it."

"No, listen."

"Now I hear it," Granddad said.

"Me too," Gran added.

"I've heard it before," Mum said. "I was a little girl...."

She struggled to remember. For several moments she frowned.

Up on the roof Pricklepot was inspecting the damage.

"What fun!" he said.

Downstairs Mum heard what he said and gasped.

"That voice. I've heard it before."

She wracked her brains.

"Will was telling the truth all along! I remember!"

She reached for her coat.

"Where are you going?" Gran said.

"I know what I have to do," Mum said. "My little boy is out there in that storm. He is trying to do the job I left unfinished all those years ago."

Without another word she rushed out into the storm. At the end of Owl Heart Lane she turned right not left. Everywhere she looked there were imps and sprites, warlocks and witches. They were smashing lamps and puncturing car tyres, tugging at phone lines and trashing gardens, spinning the road signs and

emptying the litter bins. One of the witches noticed her and pointed her out with a knobby finger.

"I know you, Holly Antrobus," she cackled. "I remember you when you were a little girl. You thwarted us then. You won't do it this time."

Mum recognised the face under the conical hat. The memories were coming back quickly now.

"I remember you too, Winnie Witchikins. I dumped you back in that hole in the ground and I will do it again."

Winnie Witchikins was furious. She started to chant a spell:

"By the powers of the thickening gloom,
send this human to a speedy doom.
Train your rage on yonder Holly,
To resist us now is simple folly,
Eye of newt and wing of bat
Turn the ninny into a….."

She never got to finish the spell. She didn't manage to say the word cat or rat or whatever she had planned. At that very moment Granddad came running down the road and swatted her away with a yard brush.

"Clear off, you warty old witch," he shouted. "Holly isn't the only one who has got her memory back. I fought you when I was a lad and I'll fight you now."

"You think you're so smart, Tommy Antrobus," the witch shrieked. "Just look at you. You're growing old, Tommy while I haven't aged at all."

"I might be getting on," Granddad snorted, "but I can still handle you and your kind. Cauldron hugger!"

"Knackety knees," Winnie taunted.

"Frognapper!" Granddad shouted back. "Run Holly. I'll keep these creatures busy for you."

"Me too," came a voice and Gran appeared, jabbing at a crowd of advancing sprites.

"Now it's Tommy's sweetheart Gertie," Winnie cackled. "It's just like old times."

Gran was still wielding her umbrella.

"I'll give you old times if you go near my daughter again."

Mum took advantage of the confusion and carried on down the road to her destination.

Chapter Ten
Mirror mirror

Pileus didn't take long to tell his tale.

"This is where Holly came the night of the great storm. She read about the underworld in her book."

Will felt stupid. Why didn't he read it to the end?

"It told her about a magic mirror, in whose surface a one-seer sees nothing and a two-seer sees little more, but a three-seer discovers life's mysteries."

"What did it tell her?"

"Why," Pileus said, "it told her how to bring the animals at the seven lodges to life. It told her how to use their power to drive the mischief-makers back into the underworld."

"Do you think that's what I should wish for?" Will asked.

"I don't think so," Pileus said doubtfully. "A three-seer doesn't copy the wishes of those who went before. A three-seer finds his own way."

"So where is this mirror?" Will asked.

"It's down there," Pileus said, pointing out the narrowest of the tunnels ahead. "Go carefully, Will."

"Thank you," Will said. "I will come back and break your chains. I promise."

Pileus sighed.

"That's what Holly said, but she forgot. Don't make a promise you can't keep, Will. It's enough for you to stop the mischief-makers. If they stay free two nights or more, no power on Earth will ever force them back down here."

Will crawled through the tunnel. There were times when he had to clear the way through the dangling roots. Eventually he reached yet another chamber and there it was, the mirror. It wasn't quite what Will expected. When he stood in front of it he couldn't see his own reflection, just a kind of boiling darkness. He peered into the murk.

"I can't see anything," he said.

Then he remembered what Pileus said. A one-seer sees nothing, a two-seer sees little more, but a three-seer sees life's mysteries. He would discover the mirror's secrets. He had to. Suddenly he glimpsed movement.

"What was that?"

He stared with all his might. The dark mist began to clear and a face appeared. He recognised it immediately. It was the brown owl that had appeared outside his window that first day.

"I know you!"

"And I know you, Will Antrobus. I've been waiting for you. Nimbus has given you an open wish. So what's it to be? What are you going to wish for?"

To Will's horror, he didn't have an idea in his head.

"I don't know."

"Think," the owl said. "You worked out where Holly went. You found the mirror and cleared the mist. You're almost there."

"But I don't know what to ask for," Will cried. "I can't think of anything."

That's when he remembered something.

"When I asked Nimbus for my own spell book, he didn't say no. He said *not yet*. That's it!"

The owl nodded.

"You don't give spell books to beginners, but you're not a

131

beginner any more, Will Antrobus. You found your way to me. So what's the wish to be?"

"Please, owl," Will said. "I want my very own spell book."

There was a flash of light and a swirl of smoke and there on the ground by Will's feet was a leather-bound book. He picked it up and started to read. He flicked through the pages until he came across the very thing.

"This isn't any kind of joke,
Give me a wizard's hat and cloak."

There was another flash of light and he was dressed from head to foot in a starry cloak. He reached up and felt the conical wizard's hat.

"Oh, this is so cool!"

"I think it's quite warm," the owl said, fluttering out of the mirror.

"Oh, don't you start!" Will said.

The owl looked a little confused.

Will was ready for more magic:

"I know the very kind of spell,
Get me right out of this well."
A split second later Will and the owl were in the thicket next to
a very startled Nimbus.
"Well, well," Nimbus said, "you do learn fast, Will Antrobus."
Will looked very pleased with himself.
"I've got a lot to do," he said, "but I will have a surprise for you
later.
I think you're going to like it."
"Oh, don't keep me in suspense," Nimbus said.
"Sorry," Will said. "I've got to go. Lead the way, owl."

Chapter Eleven
Like being a kid again

The scene in the village square was a kind of wild party. Goblins were racing each other in cars and on motorbikes. Sprites were lying on their backs in the streets pouring beer from the Bear's Paw pub down their throats. If they weren't guzzling beer, they were chomping crisps and if they weren't chomping crisps they were munching nuts. Imps trundled one another around in wheelbarrows. Witches wheeled round and round in the sky above cackling triumphantly. Here and there a warlock would discover an unwary villager and give him a pink snout and a curly wurly tail.

Mum clung to the shadows and crept past the mayhem. It wouldn't do anyone any good if she got herself spotted and turned into a cat or a rat the way Winnie Witchikins wanted. Soon she was past the square and on her way to her destination, Eagle Lodge. As she looked back she could see the witches like so many crows and ravens in the sky above the square. She could hear the chorus of cackles and guffaws. She knew that they were only just getting started. If she didn't act fast there wouldn't be much left of the village or of Kingsford and Westwich. She was also desperately worried about Will. How could she have left him down there by the river? Strangely, even though she had fled from the thicket confused and haunted by what she had seen somehow she knew he was safe there. But would anyone be safe if the mischief-makers continued to roam the countryside?

She finally reached Eagle Lodge. She unlatched the gate and walked down the path past the For Sale sign to the stone carving on the wall. Her shoes crunched on the gravel.

She ignored the lighted window. She didn't knock at the door. She hoped to be flying away on the eagle's back before the people inside knew she was there. She ran her fingers over the eagle's head, the proud beak and neck feathers.

"How could I have forgotten you?" she murmured.

Standing there, it was as if she was a little girl again, riding on the mighty eagle's back.

"Can you hear me?" she asked. "Please come to life."

Something moved, but it wasn't the eagle. A man was standing behind her.

"What are you doing in my garden?" he demanded.

He looked worried. She guessed he had already had a visit from the mischief-makers. He shone a torch on her face.

"Why, it's Holly Antrobus," he said. "I was at school with you."

"George Wilson!" Mum said. "I didn't recognise you."

"What are you doing here?" George said.

He glanced warily at the night sky.

"What's happening in the village? Somebody's cut the heads off all my roses."

"Do you remember the great storm when we were kids?" Mum asked.

George frowned.

"I remember a high wind. Why?"

"It was more than a high wind, George. It was mayhem. It was magic."

He looked at her as if she was crazy.

"Have you been drinking, Holly?"

She shook her head and stroked the eagle's stony head

135

"I rode on this fine beast once."

"Rode?" George said. "What do you mean rode? It's only a stone carving."

Mum didn't get a chance to explain. Winnie Witchikins had found her.

"There you are," Winnie cried. "Your old dad isn't here to save you this time."

George stared in disbelief.

"Who? What?" he stammered.

Winnie pointed at him.

"What to do with this silly fellow?

I'll turn him into something yellow."

Mum found herself standing next to a giant banana. The banana had George's face and his arms and legs, but he was still a banana.

"I'm a banana!" George cried. "If I ever get back to normal I am selling this house to the first person who comes along, no matter how cheaply I have to let it go,"

"Now it's your turn," Winnie chuckled, turning to Mum.

"Please eagle," Mum cried, "I need you."

Tears of frustration spilled down her cheeks.

"The time is hear, the time is now,

turn this woman into a…."

"Please!"

Her tears fell on the stone carving. Instantly, a miraculous transformation was underway. Giant wings folded Mum protectively, shielding her from Winnie Witchikin's spell. A fierce, proud eye stared at her. The eagle was free! Mum scrambled on his back the way she had all those years ago. It was like being a kid again. Together they soared into the night sky. The ascent was so powerful the draught of air knocked Winnie clean off her broomstick and she landed upside down in a pile of manure in the farm next door.

"That's it, eagle, that's it."

Mum hugged its neck.

"You remember me."

The eagle shrieked.

"Of course you do."

They were speeding across the countryside.

"Let's get the others."

Chapter Twelve
Can I do anything I want?

Will glanced at the owl.

"How much can I do?"

The owl cocked his head.

"What do you mean?"

"How strong is my magic? I mean, can I do about anything I want?"

"Don't get above yourself, Will," the owl said. "You are not all-powerful. A lot of these witches, warlocks and goblins have been practising magic for a long time. Even your friend Nimbus is an experienced magician. You are new to this game."

"Can I find out what's happening?"

"Of course."

"Can I conjure up a TV?"

The owl swooped twice round and tree and settled on a branch.

"Give it a try," he said.

Will gave it a try and there was the TV. As luck would have it, the news was on.

"Breaking news," the presenter, Emily Tang was saying. "Reports are coming in off a huge outbreak of vandalism in Kingsford, Westwich and some of the surrounding villages. Our reporter John Kerfuffle is on the scene."

"Thank you Emily," Kerfuffle said. He half-turned to allow the viewers to see the scene behind him. "This is Puddington High

Street and that is the Civic Theatre, scene of Puddington's Got Talent."

Behind Kerfuffle hundreds of people were fleeing some unknown menace.

"Let me see if I can interview one of these people," Kerfuffle said.

"Sir, Sir, can I ask you what happened in there?"

"There's some kind of creature in there," the man said.

His eyes were wide and staring.

"What kind of creature?" Kerfuffle asked.

"It's got green skin and the most wicked face you've ever seen. There he is!"

The man jostled Kerfuffle out of the way and a leering, green face filled the camera. The image rocked for a few moments then the screen went black.

"We seem to have a technical fault," Emily Tang said, looking very confused and disturbed by what she had seen. "We will return to Puddington when we can. Now over to the Sports Desk."

"What do I do?" Will said. "Hob is up to mischief in Puddington, but Mum might need me in Greengate."

"Life is about taking decisions," the owl said.

"How quickly can I get to Puddington?"

"That's up to you, Will," said the owl. "It seems to me you have two choices. I can give you a ride. Either you can yourself smaller or you make me bigger. Which is it to be?"

"Do I have to do the rhyming thing?" Will asked.

"Magic works better that way," the owl said.

"OK," Will said.

He thought for a moment.

"Finger on the magic trigger,
time to make this owl much bigger."

There was a loud crack as the branch on which the owl was

standing snapped.

"Didn't think of that, did you?" the owl asked as he picked himself up off the ground.

He was much bigger. In fact, he was an owl the size of a horse.

"No," Will said. "I hope you didn't hurt yourself."

"I only hurt my pride," the owl said.

"That's OK then."

The owl glared.

"Let's go," Will said.

"Which way?"

"Puddington," Will said. "If I know Mum, she'll be OK."

"Good call," the owl said. "If Holly the woman is half the person Holly the child was, she will do just fine."

Will climbed on the owl's back.

"What's your name, by the way? I can't just call you owl."

"Guess," said the owl.

"Well, it's got to be something cool like Featherfast or Swoop."

"No."

"Razorclaw?"

"Try again."

"Airsplitter?"

"Not even close."

"Am I getting warm?"

"You're *freezing*!"

"I give up."

"It's Ted."

"Ted? You can't have a name like Ted!"

"Why not? It's a very good name."

"But you're a magic owl. You should have an amazing name."

"I do have an amazing name."

"But it isn't a bit cool. It could at least rhyme with owl."

"What, like scoul, foul, trowel or bowel?"

Will didn't like the sound of those words at all.
"I see what you mean. OK Ted, let's go."
Ted took to the air and turned towards Puddington.

Chapter Thirteen
Storm riders

In Greengate the mayhem was reaching fever pitch. Imp and sprite, warlock, witch and brownie were battering at doors and scrambling down chimneys, tearing off tiles and breaking windows. People cowered in their homes. As the mischief-makers invaded the houses, some were forced to hide in cellars or attics. Such was the fury of the underworlders, Gran and Granddad had to retreat to their cottage. There they tried to fend off the attacking witches with yard brush and walking stick.

"Is that it?" Winne Witchikins cackled. "You are reduced to fighting us with *sticks*? You were worthy opponents when you were children. Look at you now. You are old. You have lost your magic."

Gran and Granddad knew she was right, but they shouted their defiance.

"Don't gloat too soon, you pointy-headed old bat," Gran shouted. She wrinkled her nose. "Do you know you smell of manure?"

This annoyed Winnie.

"Pointy-headed!" Winnie shrieked. "I'll give you pointy-headed, Gertie Antrobus. I'll give you stink."

Gran knew what was coming. If she didn't get out of sight Winnie would turn her into a toad or a frog, a snake, a worm, a dog.

"Come on, Tom," she shouted. "We can hide in the cupboard under the stairs."

She led the way to the cupboard. They scrambled inside and locked the door from the inside.

"These bolts won't keep them out for long," Granddad said.

"I know," Gran said.

Then she paused and thought of something.

"Tom," she said, "who has locks on the *inside* of a cupboard?"

"Somebody who wants to keep something out," Granddad said.

"Maybe we did this when we still remembered that there was danger out there. Why can't I remember? I wish I was a nine-year-old boy again."

"We were three-seers once," Gran said. "Holly might get her power back, but we are too old."

Granddad squeezed her hand.

"It's up to Holly now…and Will."

Winnie Witchikins sat on her broomstick and prepared to attack.

"What shall I do with them?" she wondered out loud. "Who has a suggestion?"

"Boil them in a cauldron," said a witch called Beryl Broomstick.

"Turn them into newts," said another called Catherine Cackleworthy.

"Now that's why I am queen of these witches like my sister Grizelda," Winnie said. "Not one of you has an ounce of imagination. We need a spell that matches the victim. What would cause them most heartache?"

"They don't like being old," Beryl said. "I heard them talking."

"That's it," Winnie said. "If they don't like being sixty years old, imagine how they would feel if I made them one hundred and sixty years old."

"Or six hundred years old," Catherine said.

"Six hundred years old, but still alive," Winnie said. "Oh, that is deliciously wicked. I'll do it."

"We've got to get them out of that cupboard first," Beryl said.

"That won't be a problem," Winnie said.

"Fittle fattle, tittle tattle,
Make those bolts wildly rattle."

Inside the cupboard the bolts started to slide back.

"Tom," Gran said, "look."

Granddad tried to stop the bolt moving.

"It's no use," he said. "The magic is too strong."

"Can't we jam something behind it?" Gran suggested.

Granddad found a screwdriver and jammed it behind the bolt, but so violently did the bolt rattle that it simply popped out. The door started to open. Winnie flew through the broken window.

"Come out, come out, wherever you are," she cackled

She swooped to the open door.

"Nothing can save you now."

She started to whip up a spell.

"Show this pair age untold,
Make them six centuries old."

All she had to do was point directly at her victims and the spell

144

would work. Beaming with triumph, she made three circles in the air. She was about to point when a shadow passed over her, then another and another and yet another until seven shadows had passed. She heard her fellow witches screaming.

"What's wrong with you ninnies?" she demanded. "Well, whatever it is, it is less important than teaching Tom and Gertie a lesson they will never forget."

She was about to point when something sharp gripped her finger. Her gaze floated upwards and she gasped. There, above her, was Holly riding the giant eagle. A gryphon had Beryl Broomstick in its clutches while a dragon was chasing Catherine Cackleworthy round the garden, roasting her bottom with its fiery breath.

"You're going back where you belong," Mum said.

Between them, the seven beasts, storm riders all, had rounded up every witch and warlock in the village and were herding them out of Greengate. The magic of witches and warlock had no effect on creatures of stone. Already the weaker mischief-makers such as sprites and brownies were beating a retreat to the well.

Chapter Fourteen
Hob the goblin

Will found the goblin king directing the mayhem in Puddington's Market Square. Bins were flying. Lampposts were toppling. Cars were driven into bollards. Anybody who didn't know what was happening soon found out. Speedng goblins chased anyone foolish enough to be out that night down the street.

"Stop this right now!" Will said in his loudest, most teacher-like voice, which was neither very loud nor very teacher-like.

Hob turned and grinned.

"Well, well, if it isn't wishing well Will."

"You're going to wish you had never met me," Will said, trying to sound braver than he felt.

"So you're a wizard now, are you?" Hob snorted. "It takes more than a book of spells to make a wizard."

Will remembered what Nimbus had said about three-seers. If he could really see deep into the way things were, he didn't need any spell book. He handed it to Ted.

"Are you sure about this?" his owl friend said.

"I think so," Will said.

He realised that sounded a bit weak.

"Yes I am," he declared, as boldly as he could.

"We'll see," Hob said. "I challenge you to a magic duel."

"Do your worst," said Will. "Do you want to do rhyming spells?"

"Is there any other kind," said Hob. "The winner is the first one to come up with a spell the other contestant can't finish."

"Done," said Will.

"I hope you know what you're doing," Ted whispered.

"Me too," Will whispered back.

He stood facing Hob wearing his starry cloak and conical hat. He wished, he wished, he wished he would be strong enough to beat this horrid goblin.

"Me first," Hob said.

He thought for a moment.

"Every single rat or mouse,
Make them all as big as a house."

Will watched the giant rodents appear. He stared at them and saw them as they should be. The words came to his lips.

"See these beasties really tall,
Make them all rather small."

In an instant they were back to normal size.

"Very good," Hob said, "for a beginner."

He scratched his chin.

"Now we start our watery pranks,
make the river burst its banks."

There was a mighty roar and the slow-moving river turned into a torrent. Soon a wall of water was building, ready to descend on Puddington. Will gazed into the surging tide and saw what had to be done.

"Now that I have used my wizard brain
I can send this flood down one big drain."

A giant hole appeared in the earth, swallowed the tidal wave and gulped it down. As soon as it had opened the hole closed again. Hob was looking annoyed.

"It's time to crush this tiresome kid.
From the sea will come...a giant squid!"

There was a terrifying squelching sound and out of the night came a huge monster with eight arms and two tentacles and a deadly-looking beak. Will's heart pounded. For a moment he glanced at Ted in panic, then he steadied himself as he saw the solution.

"There's no need to fear this giant creature,
turn it into a garden feature."

The next morning, next to the fish pond, a lady called Gwen Gollygosh would find a small pot squid among her other garden ornaments.

"Tell you what," Will said. "I will start the next rhyme. If you finish it, you win and you can use your magic on me. If you fail, I can turn you into anything I like."

Hob laughed out loud.

"I have nothing to fear from a silly, little boy."

Will recited his half of the spell.

"My spell's a thing that rhymes with orange..."

Hob was still laughing then his emerald face turned lime, then peppermint, then ghostly grey.

"the word I need is…erm…xorange!"

"There is no such word as xorange," Will cried.

"Yes there is," Hob whined.

"What is it then?" Will demanded.

"It's a…a….a kind of six legged cat, a man with two noses, a blue onion…a…a…a…"

Will conjured a dictionary.

"Find it in there," he said.

Hob tried and tried then big green tears the size of grapes fell from his eyes.

"No-o-o-o!"

"I think I get my spell," Will said.

"This wicked Hob's nasty all the time,
but he's very bad at doing rhyme.
His magic really is quite tame.
Send him back from whence he came."

A whirling tornado appeared and sucked up all the goblins and sprite, witches, warlocks and imps. Pricklepot was the last to be drawn up into the swirling wind. Ted watched the tornado vanish in the direction of the river.

"Good work, Will. You really are a three-seer. You saw what had to be done."

Chapter Fifteen
Unchained

Ted raced the tornado back to the well. Will felt the wind sting his face. He gazed down at the world rushing beneath, the church steeples and the cottages, the fields and hedges, the gleaming rivers and the winking streetlights. He breathed in the night air and smiled as the winking stars glittered above.

"I did it. I won!"

"So you did, young Will," Ted said. "So you did."

On and on they flew. They wheeled over Antrobus. Already the villagers were clearing up the mess.

"Listen," Ted said.

"What a storm!" one man was saying.

"The worst one for twenty years," a woman observed as she brushed up the broken glass on the pavement.

"You would wonder a wind could do all this."

"Have they forgotten already?" Will asked.

"They're grown-ups," Ted said. "They have forgotten how to live with magic. They are one-seers all."

"What about Gran and Granddad?"

"They're too old now," Ted answered. "They were three-seers once, but now they are two-seers at best."

"That's so sad," Will said.

He thought for a moment.

"What about Mum?"

"What about me?"

Mum's voice danced on the wind.

"Where are you?" Will asked.

"Look up."

Will raised his eyes and saw the eagle gliding above him, floating on the air currents.

"You remember!"

"You made me remember," Mum said. "See you at the well."

"Is that it?" Will asked. "Will she remember for good?"

"I'm afraid not," Ted said. "She will know that something happened, but she will never know quite what. The memory will flit into her mind for a second then vanish like gossamer. After a night's sleep she will be a two-seer just like Tom and Gertie."

"But I don't want her to forget," Will cried, tears stinging his eyes. "It's not fair."

"Who said life was fair?" Ted said.

They continued their journey in silence. Ted dropped Will off at the well.

"You'd better return me to normal size," Ted said.

Will did as he was told.

"You're one of the best three-seers I've known," Ted added before soaring into the night sky.

Will waved until his owl friend was out of sight and made his way into the heart of the thicket where Mum and Nimbus were waiting for him.

"Look at this," Nimbus said, his eyes gleaming, his cheeks glowing, his beard rippling in the breeze. "I've got two of my favourite ever three-seers together. Why don't you lift the board back on the well and keep those mischief-makers at bay for another twenty years?"

Mum took her side of the board. Will was about to take his when he remembered something.

"No," he said, "not yet. I have to go down there one more time."

"Whatever for?" Nimbus asked.

"You'll see."

"Very well," Nimbus said, "but be back before first light."

"Is it really necessary?" Mum asked.

"Oh yes," Will said.

"But what's the big secret?"

Will tapped his nose and vanished into the well. He found Pileus sitting where he had left him hours before.

"You remembered!" Pileus.

"Yes," Will said, "and I have the power to set you free."

He thought about the spell he was going to use.

"Time to think and use my brains,

Make a magic hammer to smash these chains."

A silver hammer appeared before him. Will took it in his right hand and, with one swing, broke the link in the chain next to Pileus' manacles.

"Come on, Pileus," Will said. "Let's spring our surprise."

A few minutes later he climbed out of the well. After a long night the birds were singing their dawn chorus.

"What's the big secret?" Mum asked.

"I've got somebody I want you and Nimbus to meet," Will said.

Pileus clambered out of the well. Nimbus' eyes welled with tears.

"Dad?"

"Pileus!" Mum said. "I'm so sorry. I was meant to come back for you."

"There's no need to say sorry," Pileus said. "This son of yours took up where you left off. You've got a good lad there."

Mum tousled Will's hair.

"I know."

There was a moment's silence then Nimbus took his dad in a great, big bear hug.

"Dad!"

"Son!"

"That," Mum said, "is a happy ending."

She patted the eagle.

"Get yourself home, old friend," she said.

The eagle vanished into the retreating darkness. Soon the sun appeared.

"We'd better be off," Mum said.

"Goodbye," Nimbus said, "and thank you. Thank you so much."

With that, mother and son made their way home through the meadow, across Farmer Sutch's field, over the rickety bridge and into Owl Heart Lane. Soon they would be walking down the drive of Gran and Granddad's cottage.

Chapter Sixteen
Try to remember

The lamp in Gran and Granddad's garden was winking a welcome.

Will felt sad that Mum would go to bed soon and wake up next morning, having forgotten everything that had happened.

"You won't remember anything," he said. "Nimbus told me."

"I know," Mum said. "You brought back a little girl called Holly just for one night."

"Why can't you always be like Holly?"

"Oh, Holly is inside me, but that's growing up. You change. You have new adventures ahead of you."

"Why do we have to grow up?" Will asked. "I like life just the way it is. It was so cool meeting all those stone animals and doing magic spells. Why can't I just stay exactly the way I am?"

"There is more to life than magic," Mum said.

"Magic is enough for me," Will said.

"You will think differently one day," Mum told him. "You will have other things on your mind."

They reached the drive and saw the broken chimneypot, the shards of glass that were strewn everywhere, the fallen branches.

"What a mess!" Mum exclaimed.

Gran and Granddad were out tidying up.

"What a storm!" Granddad said.

Will found it odd that neither Gran nor Granddad asked where they had been all night. He found it even odder that they had forgotten all about the mischief-makers already.

"Well, time for bed," Gran said. "You need a good nap, young man."

Will plodded upstairs to bed. He brushed his teeth and struggled into his pyjamas. He gazed out across the village before drawing the curtains. A new day was dawning. When he woke up he would be the only one who remembered the night of mayhem and who had been responsible for all the damage. After everything that had happened it was going to be such a disappointment. At least, that's what he thought, but he had one more surprise in store.

"It's a bit late for breakfast," Gran said when he made his way into the kitchen a few hours later, "but it's been a funny, old night. I'll make you some bacon, eggs and mushrooms as a special treat."

"Is Mum up?" Will asked.

"Yes," Gran said, "she only had a quick nap, unlike Mr Sleepyhead. She had somebody to meet at Kingsford station."

"Who?"

"You'll find out soon enough," Gran said.

Will wondered why she was being so secretive. He wracked his brains, trying to work out who Mum was meeting, but he couldn't think of anybody.

When he had had his breakfast, he set off towards the rickety bridge. He reached the wishing well and found Nimbus waiting for him. So was Pileus.

"We did it, didn't we?" Will said.

"Yes, we showed those mischief-makers who's the boss," Nimbus said. "And I got my old dad back."

"I wish my dad would come and see me," Will said. "I think he's fallen out with my mum."

"You never know," Nimbus said. "You might get a nice surprise one of these days."

"I don't think so," Will said. "I haven't seen him since I came to Greengate."

"Do you want to see him?" Nimbus asked.

"Of course I do. He plays football with me in the garden."

"Maybe you should wish for it."

"You said you couldn't make that kind of wish come true," Will protested.

"There's no harm trying," Nimbus said. "I never thought I would see my old dad again and you made my wish come true. Why shouldn't yours?"

"I think I will have to go back to London quite soon," Will said.

"Will I see you again next summer?"

"Next summer and the summer after that," Nimbus said. "Maybe even the one after that. Then you will start to forget us the way Holly did."

"I don't want to forget you!" Will cried.

His eyes started to sting.

"That's the way of humankind," Nimbus said. "We gnomes age slowly. It's quicker with you. Many seasons will go by before I am grey like my old dad here, but you will grow into a man, meet a wife, have children of your own in that time. Human life is short and bittersweet."

"But I will see you again next summer?" Will asked.

"Oh yes."

"Then I think I can handle all the other stuff."

"That's good," Nimbus said.

"See you Nimbus," Will said. "You too, Pileus."

"'Bye Will," said Pileus, "and thank you for setting me free."

"See you, Will," said Nimbus.

Will set off home, kind of happy and kind of sad. As he walked down the lane towards Gran and Granddad's cottage a taxi pulled up and Mum got out.

"Who were you meeting?" Will said.

Then he saw for himself.

"Dad! Does this mean….?"

"We've worked things out, son," Dad said. He sat down on the wall and Will climbed up beside him. "It's like this. I wanted to stay in London. Holly here, well, she has never been happy away from Greengate."

"But what's changed?"

"We're moving up here," Dad said. "I put in an offer for a Bed and Breakfast place up the road. The owner said the storm was the last straw. He wants to get out of here. He said something about bananas."

"Which house are we buying?" Will asked.

"Some place called Eagle Lodge."

Will glanced at Mum. Her eyes were sparkling. Maybe she did remember, just a bit.

"So you like our arrangement?" Dad asked.

"I love it," Will said. "So we're never going back to London?"

"Your mum and I will have to nip back to organise the move. You've no need to come."

Will jumped down off the wall.

"I've got somebody to tell."

"Looks like Will has made a friend here," Dad said. "Any idea who?"

Mum shook her head.

"I thought I had his name for a moment there, but it's gone."

They watched Will until he turned left towards the rickety bridge then walked inside.